Praise for

I0616874

Bend

The plot flow is smooth...plenty of twists and turns...blistering hot sexual relationship.
~ *Literary Nymphs Reviews*

...a complex love story... Its complicated plot has many emotional twists and turns... ~ *Queer Magazine Online*

...a complex romance with three engaging protagonists... The sex between this passionate trio is intense and scorching hot... ~ *Blackraven's Reviews*

Love in Xxchange

BEND

BAILEY BRADFORD

Bend
ISBN # 978-0-85715-756-0
©Copyright Bailey Bradford 2011
Cover Art by Posh Gosh ©Copyright August 2011
Interior text design by Claire Siemaszkiewicz
Total-E-Bound Publishing

BEND

Dedication

This is for the wonderful people who asked for it, and kept me going at it with the many kind comments and support.

Chapter One

"Come on, baby," Annabelle gasped, "you *know* I'll ride you hard and dirty if that's what it takes! Uhn!" Her ass hurt, her thighs were screaming, and she was being pounded within an inch of her life. She was pretty sure her internal organs had been battered and were even now free-floating in her body, her ovaries and kidneys high-fiving each other as they switched spots. "Christ!" A particularly hard slam had her teeth snapping together and black dots dancing in her vision, but she was still...hanging...on! *Take that, you stubborn, crazy —*

"Annabelle! What the fuck are you doing?" Rory yelled and diverted Annabelle's attention at the worst possible time. The horse beneath her kicked his back legs out at as he lowered his shoulders and twisted, then jerked and reared up — and Annabelle hit the dry, hard dirt with a bone-jarring thud that surely turned those floating organs into a sloppy pulp. "Annabelle! Shit! I *told* you to leave Manilo to me! He's too ornery and just too much horse for you!" Rory slid to his knees beside her, reaching for her before stopping with his hands just above her shoulders like he was afraid to touch.

He should be, Annabelle fumed, despite the pain in her body. *If he hadn't been such a damn momma about this, I wouldn't have been distracted.* As much as she'd love to point that out to him, she wasn't sure she could even breathe yet, much less light into him. Somehow she managed to sit up and suppress the shudders that wanted to rip through her. Getting thrown sucked. Getting thrown while your hovering brother watched sucked stubby monkey toes.

"Sis, how…where does it hurt?" Rory rolled his eyes at his question before Annabelle could. "Stupid question, I know. Manilo tossed you off like you were nothing, and you landed damned hard."

"No kidding," Annabelle huffed out, the words scraping her throat. Was there nowhere on her that didn't hurt? "'Cause you screeched like a momma at me, distracted me. Thanks." Geez, her chest hurt. She glared at Rory until the prancing horse behind him caught her eye. Manilo looked inordinately pleased with himself, and in case she didn't get the visual clues, he nickered and tossed his head before bolting across the corral.

Rory must have decided if she was well enough to snark at him, she was okay to touch. He grabbed her shoulders and shook her lightly. "If you hadn't got on Manilo like I told you not to, then there'd been no startling you, would there?"

Annabelle groaned and knocked his hands away. "If *you* would stop treating me like a helpless female, then you wouldn't have screeched and scared the beejeezus out of me! I'd still be on Manilo!" *Maybe.* Manilo made a sound which she was sure was the equine version of laughter and reared up. Rory's hand on her cheek brought her attention back to him. The concern in his midnight eyes, so like her own, almost made her not quite furious with him.

"I can't help worrying about you. You're the only sibling I have, the only *family*..." Rory's eyes grew damp and his lower lip trembled.

Well, crap. That always *kills my mad.* "I know, but—" Annabelle raised her hand to cup his and hissed as pain shot through her wrist. Tendrils of heat speared down to her elbow and up to her fingertips.

Rory rocked back on his heels as he chewed on his bottom lip. "You need to get checked out. Is that the worst of it, your arm...wrist?" he corrected when Annabelle shook her head. "Anything worse that would keep me from helping you up? I can call an ambulance." Rory glanced over his shoulder. "Chance!"

"No," Annabelle muttered, because everything hurt, but her wrist was definitely throbbing in a worrisome way. "No ambulance. Just my wrist is all that's hurting." She could hear the heavy thud of boot steps, knew Chance was running over after hearing Rory's frantic yell. In seconds he was there too, looming over both her and Rory. His lips twitched as he looked down at Annabelle.

"Just couldn't stay off of Manilo, could you?" Chance asked, amusement tinting his voice.

Annabelle thought she did well to refrain from an answer of 'duh'. "Obviously I couldn't stay *on* him." Then she gave Rory a withering look. "Although, maybe I wouldn't have gotten thrown if doofus there hadn't started screeching like a banshee at me."

Chance huffed out a laugh. "I'm rather fond of his, hm, screeching, myself."

"Gross," was the only answer she had for that.

"So where's the most damage?"

"My left wrist," Annabelle snapped out before Rory could answer for her. The pain was steadily increasing in her wrist, and she wasn't the type to handle pain gracefully. "And it hurts like a mother."

"I can imagine," Chance agreed. "Let's get you up and to the doctor. He can fix you up in no time. Then you and your brother can have a throw-down over whose fault it was your ass got dumped."

One of the things Annabelle loved about Chance was that he stayed out of her and Rory's disagreements. She knew he most assuredly sympathised with Rory in private, but he'd never intervened or criticised her openly, and she could respect that. Chance should be on her brother's side. Rory deserved someone who'd stand by him through any and everything after the crap he'd been through.

But it'd be nice, not that Annabelle would admit it out loud, if she had someone who would stand by her, too.

Chapter Two

The doctor's office was moderately crowded as usual, but Annabelle guessed her injury took precedent over some of the other patients. It wasn't long before she heard, "Let's get you into a room."

Annabelle nodded, not paying much attention to the petite man in vibrantly coloured scrubs who was gesturing her towards the exam rooms at the back of the clinic. Chance cupped the elbow of her uninjured arm, which still managed to make her other arm throb. His low 'Damn' snapped her out of her misery long enough to glance around for the source of Chance's irritation. Her gaze settled on the pert, plump ass covered in hot pink material smattered with cartoon characters. The owner of that ass glanced back over his shoulder at her and Annabelle felt like cursing herself. Men shouldn't be that pretty, damn it!

"Yeah, yeah, he's cute," Annabelle muttered for Chance's ears only. Too bad her own were still ringing from getting tossed off Manilo; she might have been a better judge of the volume of her voice. A snort, then a chuckle came from the hot little guy in front of her. Chance groaned and looked like he wanted to slap his hand over her mouth to prevent further embarrassment. Annabelle's cheeks burned but she shrugged it off then promptly groaned as pain speared from her shoulder to her fingertips.

"Now, that's not the kind of groan I like to hear," the smaller man said, stopping at an empty exam room. His lips were tipped up in a flirty smile and his green eyes twinkled as he winked at Annabelle. "I'm Josh. Come on and have a seat and let me check your stats real quick. You—" Josh turned that wide-eyed look on Chance, and Annabelle barely managed to stifle a snicker as Chance's lips tightened and his cheeks darkened. Twinks weren't his thing, he'd said more than once, but it was obvious he found this one a bit less annoying than most—which, of course, seemed to piss him off. Josh's eyes widened even more until he looked like a green-eyed Bambi, all innocence and confusion. "Maybe *you* should sit out in the waiting room." He turned and entered the exam room, murmuring, "Or get over yourself, sheesh."

Whether they were supposed to hear or not, they did. Annabelle felt Chance go rigid beside her. She glared at him and tugged her arm free. "Behave or you get a waiting room time-out. Think of all the screaming kids and coughing and hacking, there's all kinds of cooties just waiting for you out there."

"Sorry," Chance muttered, "guess at this rate I should have just let Rory bring you after all." He flicked a look at Josh. "Or maybe not."

"Max could have brought me," Annabelle said as she sat on the edge of the exam table, referring to Chance's foreman. Max was the epitome of laid-back, and an almost complete contrast to his more outgoing and flashy fiancé, Bo. "He's totally unaware of other people in a..." Josh turned, blood pressure cuff in hand, and seemed to be waiting for her to finish that sentence. Annabelle smiled brightly at him, only she thought it was probably more of a grimace, because she fucking *hurt* and didn't feel like putting up with this male ego bullshit on a good day, much less one where her pride and her body had both been trounced.

"He only has eyes for Bo" she finished and winked at Josh, delighting at his pinkening cheeks despite her own discomfort. "Nothing personal, Josh, but no matter how cute you are, Max wouldn't look at you twice. And Chance, here, is wrapped around my brother's—"

"I'll risk catching the plague out front," Chance said, exiting the room fast enough that it really could have been called a sprint.

"I swear I was going to say finger," Annabelle said between snickers. The cuff tightened on her arm and she forced herself to quiet down and hold still.

"I haven't been here long," Josh confided as he removed the cuff, "but I have heard of him— Chance—at the Xxchange. There's all sorts of stories about him coming in and tossing Rory—I'm guessing he's your brother?—over his shoulder and doing all sorts of wicked things to him in the parking lot. If the rumours are true, they had quite a few voyeurs watching them." He hummed softly as he measured Annabelle's pulse. "Wonder if there's anything on Youtube..."

Annabelle laughed before she could stop herself. "God, I hope not, but I'd think something like that would be more likely to be up on Xtube." She

13

shuddered and bit back a gasp. "Now I'll have to be really careful about what I download there. Ugh."

Josh leant back and gave her a questioning look. "What's Xtube?"

"Oh my god, you don't know what Xtube is?" Josh looked confused, but interested. Definitely interested. "You poor, poor man. Why don't you check it out once you get home—do *not* do it on a work computer unless you want to get fired. You can give me a call or email me and tell me what you think, if you'd like. Maybe we could be friends." She felt like she was back in elementary school, trying to navigate the minefields of popularity and friendships, but the truth was, other than her brother, Chance, Max, and Bo, she didn't have any friends here. And there were just certain things she couldn't talk to any of those guys about. Ever.

Josh smiled tremulously and nodded. "That'd be nice. I haven't really had time to make any friends, and there's some narrow-minded people out here in bumfuck Texas. And the Xxchange isn't really a place to form lasting friendships."

Annabelle snorted and rolled her eyes. "No shit. About the only lasting thing you're gonna find there is a raging case of—"

"Annabelle, what have you done now?" Dr Morrow's high-pitched tenor brought their conversation to a screeching halt. Annabelle glared up at the doctor—not too far up, the man was five-five if he was an inch, and nearly as big around as he was tall. His thinning hair was slicked back with enough grease to lube a diesel engine, and his beady brown eyes lit with an interest that never failed to make Annabelle's stomach threaten to spew its contents up. Added to the man's sheer unattractiveness and creepy interest, he was a smug ass who never failed to rile Annabelle's temper.

"*I* didn't do anything other than my job," *you smarmy bastard*. She didn't add that Rory's outburst had distracted her just long enough for Manilo to toss her on her butt. The less conversation with Dr Morrow the better, as far as she was concerned.

Dr Morrow looked at her chart and clucked his tongue. "Says here you were thrown from a horse." He glanced at Annabelle, raking her with his lusty stare which never managed to rise up past her breasts. "A pretty thing like you shouldn't be putting yourself at risk that way."

Josh muttered something that sounded suspiciously like "Fucking douchebag" before gently lifting Annabelle's injured arm. He opened his mouth to speak and Annabelle just knew whatever he was fixing to say was going to get him fired.

"You seem to have forgotten what century you're in," Annabelle sniped. "Women aren't second class citizens, we don't have to stay home and spit out babies while the big strong man earns a living. Now, either take care of this or get out of the damn doorway so Chance can take me to the hospital." Or home, that would be even better.

Dr Morrow tapped the papers on the clipboard and smiled patronisingly. "Sounds like maybe that fall addled your brain. I wasn't implying any such thing."

Annabelle could see the restraint it took for Josh to remain quiet. His sharp white teeth were doing a number on his full bottom lip. She had to defuse this situation before her new friend found himself unemployed. Annabelle didn't question her instinct to protect the pretty man, she'd always been quick to defend and even quicker to make decisions.

"I'm sure I misunderstood." The words tasted like dust in her mouth, but Annabelle forged on, giving Dr Morrow her brightest smile. "It was quite a tumble and my arm, especially my wrist, hurts like a bitch." Dr Morrow flinched at the curse word and that, right there, brightened Annabelle's mood. Poking at the idiot while playing dumb was going to be fun. There was nothing quite like messing with a man's Madonna/Whore complex. "That fucking horse kicked and reared like you wouldn't believe. Reminded me of a guy I hooked up with a while back, man was hung like a horse, too and he sure knew how to use it, you know what I mean? I was walking funny for a week—"

Dr Morrow slammed the clipboard down on the counter. "I get it! Josh, let me look at that. Go check on the patient in B."

Josh looked so reluctant and uncomfortable at leaving her alone with Dr Morrow that Annabelle nearly laughed. She'd been raised on a ranch, around men meaner and tougher than Morrow. She could take care of herself, but Josh didn't know that. It wouldn't hurt her any to ease his mind a bit.. "Will you ask Chance to come back in here? I need someone to hold my good hand since the doctor won't let you do it." She didn't, but Morrow was standing so close she could clearly see his erection pressing against his trousers through the unbuttoned lab coat. She really shouldn't goad Doctor Morrow but she was hurting and short-tempered and in no mood to put up with a pervert.

"I'll get him right now," Josh promised, looking relieved as he turned and bolted out of the exam room.

Annabelle felt a stiff, fabric-covered dick brush against the back of her left hand. That was more than she was willing to tolerate. Ignoring the pain, she turned her hand and clumsily but effectively grabbed a handful of Morrow's balls, squeezing hard enough to make the man whimper. Glaring at his sweaty red face, she added a bit more pressure.

Keeping her voice low and level, she pinned him with an angry glare. "Swear to God, I'll rip these useless balls right off your body if you *ever* touch me or rub your nasty dick on me like that again."

"Not if I rip 'em off first, you fucking piece of shit." Chance's fist caught the doctor on the chin right after the words were spoken. Morrow squealed as he flew backwards. Probably should have opened her hand just a little faster, she thought as the doctor slammed into the counters behind him.

Josh ran into the room, the rubber soles of his shoes squeaking on the tiles. "What happened? Oh shit!" He paled and his lips twitched. Chance reached for Morrow, and Annabelle and Josh both scrambled to intercept him.

"I think he got the message," Annabelle pointed out as Morrow curled up on the floor. "Let's hope he doesn't call the cops."

"Let him. He better stay right there until I can get my temper under control, you hear that, Morrow? Move and I will surely beat your perverted ass." Chance turned his dark eyed glare on her. "And you *will* file a complaint with the medical board and whoever else you need to file one with. I bet you aren't the only female around here who'd file a complaint against him."

"And I'll back you up on it," Josh offered, "and start looking for another job. Morrow wasn't limited to harassing just women or patients."

Annabelle and Chance both looked at him. Josh shrugged and blushed a pretty shade of red. "What? I didn't know what to do, and didn't think anyone would take a complaint from me seriously, and I tried finding another job but—"

"Oh, fuck it." Chance took his Stetson off and ran his fingers through his hair. "Come on, you can follow us. I got some friends at the hospital." He plopped the hat back on his head. "Besides, Annabelle's seemed to take a shine to you, and I don't want to hear her bitch about how we should have helped you out."

"Thank you." Josh gnawed on his lip and looked at the floor. "I can't follow you there, though, my car's in the shop until Wednesday. Maybe I could go then?"

Chance sighed and shook his head. "I just know I'm going to regret this somehow. Come on, you can ride with us. You *will*"—Chance added when Josh started to object—"Annabelle will make my life miserable if you don't."

Josh hesitated a moment then nodded. "Yes, okay. Thank you."

Annabelle smiled at Josh as he moved to her side and carefully cupped her injured arm. "He knows me too well. And I think Chance brought his laptop along, so we can amuse ourselves on the drive to the hospital."

Chance shuddered and started leading them from the room. "Do I even want to know how y'all will be amusing yourselves?"

Annabelle snorted. "Probably not, so I'll keep the volume off." She brightened at Chance's uneasy look.

"But I'll bookmark the page for you! I bet you and Rory would *really* enjoy this site."

"Fucking Christ," Chance muttered. "I knew I was going to regret this."

Chapter Three

"I will *not* be bitchy today," Annabelle muttered to herself as she stirred the big pot of beans. She heard a snicker behind her and turned to glare at her brother. "What?"

Rory laughed and shook his head. He walked over and draped an arm over her shoulder. "I think you're already teetering on breaking that promise. You never did handle being hurt well."

Annabelle took the spoon out of the pot and set it on the ceramic utensil holder. With her uninjured hand free, she could poke her brother in the ribs, but that would be proving his point. Instead she pasted on a smile and looped her arm around his waist. "It isn't the being hurt part that annoys me, it's not being able to do anything because of it. I hate feeling useless."

"I know, but you aren't useless, you're helping get dinner ready," Rory pointed out. "And you haven't been banned from work. Chance, Max, Bo and I are just doing the heavier stuff. Chance could have made you take off until your wrist is better."

"I'd be worried she'd kick my ass if I did that," Chance replied, his smile taking the sting from the words. "Besides, I know how Annabelle feels. I could give her a run for her money when I'm laid up."

Annabelle tickled Rory when he groaned. "I think you've just been given a not so subtle warning, bro."

"No fair tickling! I can't do it back!" Rory was gasping and laughing, and soon Annabelle and Chance were laughing as well. Annabelle felt the last of her bad mood vanish; it just wasn't possible to be pissy when Rory laughed like that. On more than one occasion, Annabelle had wished she was more like her brother. Sure, they looked as alike as siblings who were of opposite sex could, but Rory truly had the personality to match his angelic face. Whereas she...didn't. Of course, he wasn't so angelic when they were butting heads, but even then he was usually only trying to protect her. And she...well she always went for the balls, didn't she? No middle ground, just full-out fury and the need to win. Her mood plummeted again just as someone knocked on the door.

"I'll get it." Annabelle slipped out of the kitchen, leaving Rory and Chance staring at each other like two love-struck teenagers with more hormones than sense. The bite of jealousy she felt didn't help her mood at all, but seeing Josh's nervous grin through the screen door did.

"Joshie! About time you got here!" Annabelle pushed the door open and tackled Josh before he could come in. His firm, muscled body felt really good pressed against her own softer one. He hugged her back with a surprising strength. For some reason Annabelle's eyes started to burn. It just felt so nice to have someone hold her, even as a friend, for a brief moment.

"I'm a little nervous," Josh whispered against her ear. "I mean, I changed outfits like seven times, trying not to look like a twink since I'm walking into the twink-monster's lair."

Laughing, Annabelle leant back, keeping her arm around Josh's shoulder. He left one arm around her hips and gestured to his clothes. "So, whaddaya think? Am I a twink in prep's clothing or what?"

Annabelle gave him a thorough once over. He was wearing a beige—beige!—button-up, tucked in to baggy khakis. Some awful-kind-of-loafers were on his feet. Annabelle wasn't so sure he was wearing them as she suspected the ugly fuckers were actually a pair of alien parasites that had attached themselves to her new best friend's feet and were, even now, sucking the fashion sense right out of him. She darted a look at his hair and cringed before she could stop herself. Josh frowned, his shoulders slumping as he reached up to pat at the heavily slicked back strands. Not a single hair moved.

"Too much?"

"Is that—" *a helmet?* Annabelle bit the words back at Josh's apprehensive look. "Are you really that nervous?"

Josh bobbed his head. "Yeah. You're the only friend I have here, the only friend I've had in a long time, really, and I don't want..." He swallowed loudly. "If they hate me, then it might be... You might not want to have anything to do with me, if it causes problems with your brother and his partner."

Annabelle snorted and gave Josh another one-armed hug, wondering about his lack of friends and confidence. He'd seemed so self-assured when she'd met him, but maybe that was his work persona. "First off, Rory doesn't get to pick my friends, neither does Chance or anyone else. Second, they'll love you anyway. Chance can be a bear, and maybe he has a reputation for not liking twinks, but that's just a label, it isn't *who* you are. Don't let what other people think shape you, okay? If someone looks at you and forms an opinion based on how you look rather than the kind of person you are, then fuck 'em, they aren't worth your time." That was one lesson she'd learned well herself.

Josh gave her a half smile and rubbed at his stiff hair. "You're right, I know that. It's just hard sometimes…" He puffed out his cheeks and exhaled in a huff. "So, overkill, then. Can we fix it?"

Annabelle glanced past Josh and spotted Max and Bo heading over from the bunkhouse. "Sure we can. Come on!" Switching her hold on Josh into a firm grip on his hand, she rushed him to the bathroom, ignoring Chance and Rory's curious stares as they bypassed the kitchen. Within moments, and with the help of the detachable showerhead, Annabelle had the goo rinsed from Josh's hair. A quick hit with the blowdryer and just a small amount of gel, and she could see the cute guy from the doctor's office emerging.

"Now, take off your shirt."

Josh looked startled for a second, then he unbuttoned the shirt and handed it to Annabelle. His white T-shirt was tight and showed off his chiselled abs beautifully. Annabelle stroked her hand over them in appreciation, knowing Josh wouldn't take it as a sexual move.

"It should be a crime to hide those things away. Come on, Josh, time to meet the crew." Annabelle held out her hand. Josh took a deep breath and pasted on a smile that only looked half-forced.

"All right, let's do this," Josh muttered. "But next time, I get to choose where we hang out."

From the wicked glint in his eyes, Annabelle had a feeling she knew where they'd be going, and damned if that didn't chase off the lingering bits of her gloomy mood.

* * * *

"Come on, relax," Annabelle coaxed. "I promise not to let any of them eat you."

"Relax, she says," Josh muttered as he let himself be lead out to the back patio. As soon as the sliding glass doors opened Josh would swear he could feel everyone's eyes on him. He was half-scared to peer around Annabelle and see if he was right. Annabelle took the choice from him, tugging with her good arm—and damn, the girl was strong—pulling him right up beside her. Josh was so nervous he didn't think to watch where he was going, which was why he tripped over the door's track guide. Of course he just *had* to catch his toes on it. He stumbled and slammed into Annabelle's back, sending them both into a frantic fight against gravity.

Annabelle only had one good arm to flail, as her sprained wrist was currently held immobile with a sling. Josh knew he was going down, just as he knew if the other people gathered outside hadn't been looking when he and Annabelle first opened that damned door, they were certainly looking now. Which would figure, since Josh landed on his ass hard enough to rattle his brains. He threw his hands up in time to catch Annabelle, or, more accurately, two handfuls of her ass.

"Oh shit, ohshitohshit!" Josh's arms gave out, driving back until his elbows smacked into the wood deck. His hands were still firmly in place, which was how he stopped Annabelle from falling onto him — at least until his sweat-slicked skin began sliding against the deck. Josh's arms wobbled and he tried to steady them but it was no use. He couldn't seem to control his own body. There was no way this was going to end well; he was already mortified and his strength was vanishing rapidly. Another wobble of his arms combined with more sweat, then Josh's elbows slid and Annabelle landed ass-first on his chest, knocking the breath from his lungs and sending tendrils of pain shooting out from his sternum.

Maybe he'd die — some bone chip would spear his heart and put an end to this whole humiliating afternoon. His ex hadn't called him a drama queen for nothing. Josh shut his eyes and tried to breathe, hearing nothing other than the pounding of his heart. Maybe Annabelle had landed with enough force to shove that organ into his head. Annabelle's weight suddenly vanished from his chest and Josh finally sucked in some air. If he whimpered a little when he did so, Josh figured it couldn't possibly make him look less a fool to Annabelle's family and friends.

"You okay?" A big hand grabbed Josh's shoulder and shook him. Josh's teeth clacked together and he swallowed the snarl threatening to bubble out. What kind of idiot would think trying to snap his head off his shoulders would be a *good* thing? Josh pried his eyes open and found himself looking at a male version of Annabelle...a really large male version. *Rory, then.* Dark blue eyes laced with a liberal dose of concern stared back at Josh. "It was kinda shitty of Annabelle to pay you back for breaking her fall by trying to crush the life outta you."

Josh snorted and groaned when the sudden jerky motion it caused in his chest sent a lick of pain through him.

Rory frowned. "Do you need an ambulance? Did Annabelle break you?"

Josh blinked and noticed more faces had appeared. He recognised Chance but there was an older man with a sun-creased face and dark eyes, and another man also older, less fine lines and wrinkles, but his hazel eyes looked older than they should. Rory's frown deepened and Josh realised he hadn't answered Rory's question.

"She didn't break anything." Josh's next breath was easier, the pain slipping away and leaving him with nothing else to focus on but his embarrassment. "And it was my fault. I tripped going out the door."

Rory's lips twitched and he arched a brow. "Are you naturally graceful, or do we make you nervous?"

Cheeks stinging, Josh nodded. "The last one, yeah."

"Huh." Rory transferred his hold to Josh's hand. "Must be Chance's mean glare. He thinks it makes him look all sexy and studly. Ready to get up?" Josh nodded and started to rise, only to stop when it occurred to him people would need to step back and give him some room rather than loom over him.

Chance tugged at one of Rory's blond curls, making the man snicker. "I didn't glare at him once we left that doctor's office. All right, back up people."

"Uh huh, but you did before then, right?" Rory stood and pulled Josh up with him. "Just 'cause he's young and cute, no doubt. Thought I broke you of that." Chance mumbled something Josh couldn't hear and wrapped an arm around Rory's hips. The look the two men shared caused a totally different kind of pain in Josh's chest. He wanted someone to look at him like that, wanted to see his love reflected back in his lover's eyes. His ex had told him more than once that men didn't love each other, not like that, they just weren't capable of it. Josh had been afraid it was true, but now, seeing Rory and Chance—hope flickered to life inside him, warming him and bringing a smile to his face.

Annabelle stepped in front of him, patting his cheek and then his chest with her good hand. Josh grunted when she prodded at his chest. "Little sore there," Josh pointed out. Annabelle crossed her eyes at him and took his hand again.

"Well of course," Annabelle agreed. "Now I know just where to poke if you get out of line, Joshie."

"Joshie?" Chance snickered and shook his head. "Christ, Annabelle, why don't you just go ahead and neuter the poor kid instead. Gotta be less embarrassing than having it done verbally."

Josh couldn't quite bring himself to glare, but he did manage to look Chance in the eye. "I *like* it when *she* calls me Joshie. Anyone else..." He trailed off, not really sure how to make that into a threat. Wasn't like Chance or Rory couldn't stomp his ass in the ground. Probably. Josh glanced at the other two men and found them both watching Chance with big smiles on their faces.

"Anyone else calls him Joshie, and I'll castrate *them*," Annabelle announced in a sing-songy voice. "With my fingernail file. He's *my* Joshie." Annabelle tapped her index finger against her chin. "You know, I should probably come up with nicknames for all of you—"

"Gotta check on the steaks," Chance muttered.

"I'll help," Rory added quickly. "Make yourself at home, *Josh*."

Annabelle turned to look at the other two men. "Max? Bo? Don't even try to run off."

Josh snickered as the two men stopped their retreat, doing a one-eighty and returning to stand by Josh. Annabelle introduced them, and Josh soon found himself relaxing and enjoying their company, even if he did feel a little jealous now and then. It wasn't a mean sort of jealousy, not at all. Josh would rather see the love flowing between Max and Bo, and Chance and Rory, than not, and even if he didn't ever find that for himself, at least now he had cause to look for it, hope for it.

"Makes you a little envious, doesn't it?" Annabelle asked with a wistful note in her voice. "Like there's maybe someone out there who can love you as you are, flaws and all."

Josh slipped his arm over Annabelle's shoulders. "Annabelle, any man — straight man, I mean — would be lucky to have you like that. Probably even some of the not-so-straight ones, too."

Annabelle shook her head and stared down at her lap. "I don't know, Joshie. I'm stubborn, and mean, and never know when to quit. I don't see how that would make me a prize."

Josh frowned so hard he felt a headache start up in his temples. Who'd told Annabelle that load of shit? Or that any of it was a bad thing? Even being mean had its place, and, while he hadn't known her very long, he had yet to see Annabelle be mean when there wasn't a good cause for it. And it wasn't really mean — if she was a man, it would have been called assertive or aggressive, but put those same qualities in a woman and that woman was a bitch. As far as double standards went, it was one of the worst. Josh shelved his anger and questions for now and used his other hand to press Annabelle's head to his shoulder.

"You're the best woman I've ever known, the best person for that matter," Josh whispered, brushing at Annabelle's curls. "And no matter what line of bullshit someone else has told you, you *are* a prize, and a treasure, and everything someone could want in a lover."

Annabelle huffed and looked up at him with watery eyes. "Not everything. I've got the wrong parts for you."

"You wouldn't want me anyway," Josh told her. "You need someone as strong as you are, and I would never have had the nerve to grab Doc's balls like you did. You're my hero." As Annabelle laughed, the sadness leaving her dark eyes, Josh decided he'd do what he could to help Annabelle find her special someone. "Maybe we should go out tomorrow, hit up a club or two." Not that he wanted Annabelle to find some hook-up in a meat market, but it'd be good to get her out, make her laugh, let her see how many men were interested. He just wouldn't let any of them touch her. Later he'd figure out how to put his plan into motion.

"We could go to the Xxchange."

Josh nudged Annabelle's head with his shoulder. "That's a gay bar. I was kind of thinking we could go to Barking at the Moon or somewhere like that."

Annabelle gave him a look that told him she knew what he was thinking. "And I was thinking the Xxchange."

"Oh." Josh tipped his head up and watched a fat white cloud roll by. Annabelle was trying to find *him* that someone special! "I doubt lightning will strike twice. Just 'cause Rory and Chance met there and found their happily-ever-after doesn't mean I will. That place was definitely a fuckstop."

"What's a fuckstop?"

Josh cringed and looked at Chance, who was now standing in front of him, Rory pressed to his side. "Uh...a place where you stop to get fucked? 'Cause it's pretty much a sure thing? Like, uh, some clubs."

"Like the Xxchange," Rory said, chuckling as Josh felt his cheeks flame. "That where you were talking about?"

"I..." Josh really wanted that bone chip to take him out, any time now. "Maybe?" Chance's bland expression made Josh babble. "Yes? But I didn't mean anything bad, just that it's not a place a guy goes to find anything more than a quick—uh, unless he gets lucky, like you two did, and chances of that happening again aren't good, so—"

Bo walked over with Max at his side. "Josh has a point. I spent years in places like that and never found anyone interested in more than a one-off. Course, now I have Max, and he was sure worth waiting for."

Max blushed a deeper red than Josh ever had, but his eyes gleamed with happiness and his lips curled up in a sweet smile. "Bo..."

"You know it's true, sweet man," Bo crooned, kissing Max noisily. "I have to brag about what a great guy I have, don't I?"

Annabelle made a gagging noise as she sat upright. "Okay, all this mushy shit is getting a bit nauseating for us poor singles. I think me and Joshie are going to get out of here for a bit. Come on, let's leave before they start doing something gross like having a big gay orgy or singing and doing the Macarena."

Laughing, and a little worried about what plans Annabelle might be coming up with, Josh said his goodbyes quickly but sincerely and followed Annabelle inside.

Chapter Four

Annabelle pulled up in front of Josh's apartment at nine o'clock sharp. She checked the parking lot carefully, looking for any signs of danger. There was only one flickering streetlight in the vicinity, and the neighbourhood was run-down. All in all, the place was more than a little creepy. Maybe now that he'd been hired at the hospital, Josh could move to a nicer place once the lease here was up. Annabelle had been inside his apartment exactly one time before and while he kept the place immaculate, it was still a total, complete dump.

She toyed with the idea of asking Chance to let Josh live in the bunkhouse with her, Max and Bo. Josh could pay rent since he wouldn't be working at the ranch and Annabelle wouldn't have to worry about someone murdering her best friend while he slept. Chance would probably go for the idea if for no other reason than to shut her up, and Rory, Max and Bo all seemed to like Josh. It was hard not to when he was such a charming mix of bravado and humility. Being so cute didn't hurt any, either. But, getting Josh to agree might prove difficult as he also had a stubborn streak in him and a need to prove himself, although Annabelle hadn't managed to pry that story out of him. Yet.

After a last slow check of the area, Annabelle shut off the engine and got out of her truck. She grabbed her cell phone from where it'd fallen under her seat. A glance at the screen showed half a dozen missed calls, all from Josh. Annabelle felt worry coil in her gut as she locked her door and slammed it shut. Maybe Josh had only been calling for clothing advice — six missed calls didn't have to mean there was anything horribly wrong.

"Fuck it." Annabelle shoved the phone in her back pocket and ran across the street to the apartments, cursing the fact that the place had such a miniscule parking lot as each renter was only assigned one slot. The few dozen unassigned ones had already been taken by the time she'd arrived.

Annabelle took the stairs two at a time, not giving a shit if her boots pounding on the cement steps shook the whole building. No one in their right mind should be asleep this early on a Saturday night anyway. She bounded up the last two steps and took a right, running the ten feet to Josh's door. Raising her hand to knock, she heard voices in the apartment, angry tones though she couldn't make out the words. Whoever was in there with Josh was obviously pissed off about something, and her imagination began tossing out all sorts of violent scenarios. Annabelle pounded on the door three times and kicked it once for good measure when she heard Josh's voice, the anger in it firing her own temper.

"Someone better open this goddamn door before I call the police!" Annabelle didn't give them time to let the threat sink in. She smacked the door again. "Joshie! Are you okay?"

She heard Josh holler "Don't!" then the front door was swinging open. Annabelle had started to beat on the door again and blinked with surprise when her fist connected with a broad, muscled chest. Too worried about Josh, she slapped both hands against that firm flesh, and, grimacing a bit at the pain that speared out from her injured wrist, Annabelle shoved that broad chest hard, putting her weight behind it. The man must not have expected a woman her size to make such a move or have such strength. He gave a startled sound and stumbled backwards as Annabelle shoved by him and bolted into the apartment. Her eyes locked with Josh's. Finding nothing more than anger in his gaze, she swept a glance over him.

"You okay, Joshie?" Annabelle hurried to his side and hugged him, relieved to feel his arms immediately lock around her waist. She felt Josh rub his cheek against her temple, his soft sigh sending his breath tickling over the fine hairs that had slipped loose from her French braid.

"I'm fine, Annabelle," Josh said softly, sounding so tired it made her heart ache. "It's just—"

"Joshie?"

Josh tensed against her. Annabelle pulled away far enough to turn her head and glare at the man who'd spoken. She supposed the big jerk was the man who'd answered the door, just as she supposed the tingling she felt all over was from being mad enough to gouge the guy's eyes out. It had nothing to do with the fact that he was gorgeous in that lived in, roughhewn way. Ignoring the fact that the tingling seemed to be strongest in her nipples and pussy, Annabelle turned fully to face the other man.

Goddamn it! Everything about the man hit every one of her hot buttons — except for the way she'd heard him yelling at her best friend and the astonished, mocking tone in his voice when he'd repeated Joshi's nickname. Those things were reason enough to smother the heat she'd felt seconds earlier.

Cocking her head to the side, Annabelle gave the big man her haughtiest look. "Yeah, Joshie. Get over it. I have several names for you if I need them." *Sexy bastard* would be at the top of the list, but as Annabelle looked the man over from boots to brim, not caring one whit if it was rude or not, she thought that might not be an adequate description.

Tall, broad and built, his Wranglers hugging thickly muscled thighs, his cock a large, luscious offering encased in denim, and narrow hips she'd love to feel slamming against her ass or pounding against her spread thighs… That tingling returned, ramping up to an inferno as Annabelle took in the flat stomach and broad chest. She wished he was wearing a T-shirt instead of buttoned up denim, she'd really like to see those muscles.

By the time she dragged her gaze up to his face, she was glad she'd decided not to forego wearing underwear tonight, that thin layer of silk was probably all that was keeping her from soaking her jeans with her happy juices.

Then again, that smirk on the handsome face might just be the cause of her utter humiliation. Full lips stretched wide, the move bringing up deep dimples in the man's cheeks. Annabelle said a silent prayer of thanks to the DNA gods. This man had it all — sharp blades of cheekbones, a long, narrow nose with the slightest bump in the bridge, and large, light brown eyes that glittered with amusement. The brim of the Stetson kept her from getting a good look at the man's eyebrows or hair colour, but she'd bet a week's pay it was some hot as hell shade of brown.

"Do you need some more time, make sure you didn't miss anything?" The man asked in a baritone that sent a shiver down her spine. Annabelle's irritation returned full force at the smugness in that deep voice.

"Nope. Seen enough and heard enough to know you're an ass."

The man looked startled for half a second then he chuckled. The rich, warm sound only pissed Annabelle off more as she turned back to Josh. "Who is this jackass, and why is he hassling you?"

She ignored the laughter from behind her, figuring she did well not to toss the big jerk the bird. Josh studied her, frowning intently as footsteps pounded up the stairs. She thought there was a warning in her best friend's eyes, but a warning for what, she couldn't tell. Josh sighed and turned her around in his arms. He flopped a hand at the big man.

"Annabelle Calhoun, meet my brother, Justin Taylor."

I will not be embarrassed. He was being a jerkoff to Joshie! "That doesn't make him less of an ass for yelling at you." She wasn't going to budge on that. She'd file him away in her brain as Justin/Asshole. Annabelle glared as Justin grinned.

"And that," Josh nudged her shoulder with his own, drawing her attention to a shape in the open doorway, "is Justin's partner, Evan Ross."

Well, fuck, of course.

Bend

Chapter Five

Evan was every bit Justin's equal in attractiveness. Long and leanly muscled, he was less bulky. His straight black hair hung to his shoulders. A clump of bangs flopped over one of his pale blue eyes. He had a pert nose and pale skin, warmed by the pink tinting his cheeks. His top lip was thin but elegantly shaped, topping off the lower, plumper one in a way that made Annabelle want to suck on the full pink flesh. Then he smiled, and Annabelle felt her heart stutter and her core pulse.

"Hi," Evan said tentatively in a soft voice. She felt Josh's arms stiffen around her briefly, then he released her and muttered something she couldn't make out.

"You must be Annabelle," Evan continued, walking slowly into the apartment as if afraid she'd do him bodily harm. She might, just probably not the kind he was worried about. Evan shut the door and took a few more steps inside. "Josh has told us about you. I'm glad he has such a good friend here."

Annabelle refrained, barely, from informing him Josh hadn't mentioned either of them to her at all. She wasn't sure what that meant, and would prefer to find out from Josh later when the other two men were gone. Annabelle crossed her arms over her chest and tapped the toes of one boot on the nappy vinyl flooring. She glared from Evan to Justin then back at Evan.

"What is this, good boyfriend bad boyfriend? Justin's the jerk, and you're the nice one?"

Evan's brows shot up his forehead as Justin narrowed his eyes at her. Seemed his tolerance for her smart mouth had run out. Annabelle gave him a look, daring him to say something about it. When Justin's lips only thinned into a line, she faced Evan again, tapping her toes faster, hoping the pop of the boot on the floor would burn off some of the emotions swirling in her gut, among other places.

Evan glanced at Justin questioningly then looked at her and shrugged. "I guess he can be abrasive sometimes."

Annabelle heard Josh's snort even as she made the same noise. Justin started to say something only to be cut off by Josh.

"Try bossy, demanding, and convinced he's always right." Josh stepped to Annabelle's side, fisting his hands on his hips. "And he always knows what's best for everyone else, especially me."

Annabelle cringed inwardly. That kind of sounded like a description of her. She looked at Justin to see his reaction and thought she must have been wrong. Surely that hadn't been a flicker of hurt in those golden eyes.

"Josh," Evan said, reaching out with one hand as if to stop the flow of anger between the two brothers.

"Justin is just worried about you. He said he was only going to offer to move you into a nicer neighbourhood, somewhere with a good security system—" Evan stopped and gave Justin a worried look as Annabelle felt a sinking in the pit of her stomach. Hadn't she had those same concerns, many times over?

"That *is* all you told him, right?" Evan asked Justin. Justin crossed his arms over his chest and nodded. Annabelle didn't miss the way she and Justin held themselves in similar positions. It irked her, even if it was a childish reaction, and she had to force herself not to drop her arms back to her sides. She pinned Justin with a narrow-eyed look and stopped tapping her toes.

"If that was all you were doing, why were you yelling at Joshie?" She saw Evan jerk and mouth "Joshie?" silently and gave him her best I-will-kick-your-ass look. Evan snapped his mouth shut.

"Because he said no," Justin muttered. "He'd rather stay here in this death trap instead of letting me help him out."

Oh shit shit shit! Annabelle felt her cheeks burning. She'd planned on having the same argument with Josh as soon as possible—and she'd known it would be an argument, that Josh wouldn't want to accept any help. He'd only let Chance help him get a job because he'd had no other choice, not after walking out on doc perv. Annabelle looked at Josh and saw the stubborn set of his jaw. The man might look sweet as cotton candy, but she knew he had a temper.

"I don't need or want any more handouts!"

Justin ground his jaw for a second then said slowly, as if speaking to a child, "I offered to set it up as a loan then, and let you pay me back in instalments. I don't see why that's such a horrible thing to do or so hard for you to accept—"

"Because I can make it on my own," Josh said, sounding so much like his brother Annabelle barely kept from gaping at him. There was nothing of the sweet man she knew in his countenance now. "I don't want any help from you *or* Evan. Jesus, cut the damn apron strings already, Mom."

Annabelle swung her head back around to see Justin's reaction, certain he'd have a sharp retort for Josh. Sure enough she saw anger flicker across his face, but then Evan was beside him, one arm over those broad shoulders, murmuring quietly in Justin's ear. Justin tensed briefly, then his shoulders drooped as his arms dropped to his sides. He nodded once, his gaze darting from Josh to Annabelle. Annabelle found herself pinned by the look in his eyes, something dark and sensuous that fuelled a need she'd been keeping buried deep inside.

She knew that look, had seen it other men's eyes. Justin wanted to fuck her, pound out the anger and frustration he was feeling by burying his cock in her warm, willing body. Except she wasn't willing, not when Justin had a partner.

Turning to Josh, she missed the look on Evan's face, a nearly identical one to Justin's.

"Are y'all done here?" Annabelle asked her friend. "The band is supposed to start any time now, and I'd really like to catch some of their show. Dancing would be good, too." Maybe she could find someone to help her work off a bit of stress. The Xxchange had to have at least a few bi guys in it. There'd certainly been several there when she'd been with Bo and Max; Annabelle hadn't missed the lusty looks she'd received. That was why she'd chosen the place for tonight's night out. There was a more than decent chance both she and Josh would get laid.

"I know I'm done, just let me get dressed." Josh started to walk to the bedroom. Annabelle grabbed his arm and waited until he looked at her.

"Wear the tight purple shirt and those ripped jeans we got at the mall. The make your ass look irresistible." She glanced down to see what shoes he was wearing and cringed. "And dump those sandals. Shit, burn 'em. Wear the black biker boots. You'll have every guy in the place panting after you."

Josh blushed in the way Annabelle found adorable. He glanced at something over her shoulder then back at her. "Okay, got it. Put on the 'fuck me' outfit." Josh gripped Annabelle's uninjured arm in return and began dragging her to his room. "But you have to wear one, too. Come on."

"What?" Annabelle blanched at the squeaked out word. She forgot about Josh's guests as she tried to dig in her heels. "What the hell is wrong with my jeans and tank top? And my boots, I'm a cowgirl—"

"Not tonight you aren't," Josh interrupted. "Tonight you're gonna be the hottest damn woman in Texas, possibly the whole world." He jerked on her arm and ignored her cussing and the way she was dragging her feet.

Annabelle gave up and let Josh have his way. Maybe it'd soften him up and he'd be willing to accept an offer to live in the bunkhouse if she played this right. It wouldn't be a lie to point out all the fun they could have if he lived with her, but they'd probably drive Max and Bo nuts. She grinned at the thought. It'd be good for those two, Max and Bo needed a little shaking up every now and then. So did Rory and Chance. Those four were going to turn into those dull couples whose idea of a wild night was playing bingo at the community centre. She'd make Josh see what a great idea it was without going at it from the same angle Justin had. Good thing he'd tried that one first. Now Annabelle knew to stay away from the whole 'Josh, I'm worried about your safety' thing.

"Ta da!" Josh bounced on his toes and waved at a garment lying on his bed. "And there's shoes, too, right" — he bent and pulled a box from under his bed — "here!"

Eyeing both items with a tinge of trepidation, Annabelle approached the bed and began opening the garment bag. There was, she noted, quite a bit more bag than garment. She laughed as she saw what Josh had picked out for her then turned and hugged him, nearly toppling them both. It looked like Josh had the same plan she'd had — to get his best friend laid, and damned if she didn't think they would both succeed.

Chapter Six

"You want her." It wasn't a question, Evan knew his lover well enough to pick up on the signs, and even if he hadn't, he'd have to have been blind to miss them. Justin was flushed from the open collar of his shirt up to where the brim of his Stetson set on his brow. His lips were darker, parted, his nostrils flaring slightly with each breath. His big body was tensed, the muscles coiled as if he were holding himself back from slamming Annabelle on the floor and burying his cock inside her. Fisted hands, erection straining in his jeans—yeah, Evan knew the signs, and since he felt the same way himself, he only smiled when Justin opened his mouth to deny it.

"She *is* an interesting mix," Evan continued as he glanced at Josh's bedroom door. "Face of an angel, mouth of a sailor—" an image of those full red lips flashed in his mind. "Well, language of a sailor, that mouth is definitely made for sin," he corrected. "Temper that sparks and ignites in a snap, and that body…" Evan palmed his own aching dick as Justin grunted.

"Yeah, and she obviously thinks I'm the devil himself," Justin pointed out. "That last look she gave me nearly singed my balls off, and not in the way I'd have liked."

Evan snorted and plopped down on the ratty couch. "Well, you were eye fucking her, and she knows we're a couple, what'd you expect? She probably thinks you're a whore and I'm an idiot for putting up with it."

Justin humphed and gingerly sat beside Evan. "You were drooling, too."

Evan snickered and danced his fingers over Justin's cock. "Well, yeah, but I didn't get caught."

"Oh fuck," Justin groaned, his hand trapping Evan's against his groin. "Stop or I'm gonna make a mess." Actions contrary to words, he thrust into Evan's hand. "Fuck—Ev—" Justin's lids dropped down and he hissed, the air whistling past his clenched teeth.

Evan cupped Justin's length, rubbing the heel of his hand hard against it like he knew Justin needed him to. Justin shuddered and groaned, his big body clenching then going still as he struggled for control. Evan toyed with the idea of making his lover come; Justin in climax was a sight to behold. Evan had fallen in love with the man the first time he'd watched him come, his thick cock shoved into Evan's mouth, the tip buried in his throat. Evan had been so entranced he'd nearly choked, forgetting to swallow the load of spunk.

Laughter—Josh's and Annabelle's—rang out from the bedroom. Evan's skin heated with need at the sound of Annabelle's infectious laugh even as a trill of fear wound into his spine. He found himself drawn back to Justin, unsurprised at the knowing look in the man's eyes. Justin studied him closely. Evan tried to hide his fears but his lover knew him too well. In the blink of an eye, Evan was embraced in Justin's arms, his slighter body pulled up tight to the bigger man's.

"We don't have to, if you're not ready yet," Justin whispered the words against Evan's skin, his moist breath warming Evan, chasing back memories that still made Evan's heart ache.

"Josh would probably hate me anyway if..." But Evan knew Josh hated him anyway, Justin just didn't seem to see it. While Evan really didn't want there to be discord between the two brothers—more discord, that is—he hadn't seen Justin ever react as strongly to a potential third as he had Annabelle. Then again, Evan hadn't been so tempted before, either. Yet he knew, despite his and Justin's reactions to Annabelle, all he had to do was say 'no' and Justin would honour his decision.

The thing was, Evan wondered if Justin wouldn't resent him for it eventually. They'd agreed from the beginning that, as much as they fit, they needed a woman to complete their relationship. It'd taken a while for them to figure out one-night stands weren't fulfilling for either of them; they wanted someone permanent, someone who wanted more than just the thrill of fucking two guys at once. A surprising number of women had been open to trying it once, but mention a relationship, and most of them thought he and Justin were nuts.

As for Josh...Evan frowned. That was something Justin had to decide. Josh had been more than clear on his feelings about Evan—he didn't matter. Period.

Justin smoothed his thumb over Evan's brow, humming softly. "Josh didn't have a problem with Amanda, until the end."

Evan didn't even ask how Justin had known what he was worrying about. The man just *did*. "Yeah, but Mindy wasn't his BFF to begin with. He only tolerated her because of you."

"And he hasn't known Annabelle for all that long." Justin shrugged, his breath hitching when Annabelle's laughter rang out again. "Besides which, he told me people should love who they love and it wasn't anyone else's business how that went down. I think, if Annabelle's interested, or if we can get her interested, it should be her choice we are concerned with, not my brother's. He'll come around if she's happy."

"Huhn." Evan wasn't too sure about that. If nothing else, Josh would hate for Annabelle to be with him. Still, Justin obviously thought Annabelle was worth taking a risk on and Evan, even though he was terrified after Mindy, *was* extremely attracted to Annabelle. He looked into Justin's eyes, seeing the love and acceptance that had never faltered in their years together, not even when they were both plunged into despair. He'd do anything for the man who looked at him like that, and when it was something Evan wanted as well...

Evan saw the subtle shift in Justin's expression and knew his lover had read the answer in Evan's eyes before Evan spoke. "I think, if we can convince Annabelle, she just might be the woman we've been looking for." He only wished he wasn't absolutely terrified by the truth of those words. Then Annabelle came out of Josh's bedroom and Evan forgot his worries. He couldn't think past the blood roaring in his ears, rushing to his dick as Annabelle turned her heated gaze on him.

"Holy shit."

"Holy shit indeed," Justin muttered.

* * * *

Annabelle might have laughed at Josh's declaration that Justin *and* Evan had both been 'drooling like idiots' over her, but she wasn't laughing now. When Josh had warned her in his bedroom about his brother and Evan's tastes, she'd been intrigued, but figured her friend had it wrong. She'd convinced herself she'd misunderstood the look Justin had given her before she'd been dragged off so Josh could play fairy godmother. After all, the fire in Justin's eyes could very well have been nothing more than temper, and she hadn't seen Evan's expression. But Josh had, and Annabelle had found herself in the position of being warned about dangerous men and protecting her virtue. She'd laughed so hard she'd nearly peed.

Then she'd stepped out of Josh's bedroom wearing what amounted to a scrap of hot pink material that barely covered up her fun bits and mile-high fuck-me shoes splashed with bits of sparkly silver. Her hair had been freed from its 'prison', as Josh referred to her French braid, and finger-combed until it gleamed like waves of pale moonlight down to the top of her ass. Josh had bemoaned her makeup skills, then grabbed a bag from his dresser drawer. Annabelle didn't even want to know why he had a makeup bag. By the time he was done with her, she'd felt like a different woman, and that was fine, being feminine was okay at times—but it was especially okay when it left two gorgeous men gaping at her like they wanted to toss her down and eat her up.

Josh had snarled and pretty much dragged her from the apartment. Annabelle had only balked when he'd tried to get her to agree to take one vehicle. No way was she leaving her truck in this shithole of a neighbourhood.

Justin and Evan hadn't been far behind them, and while Annabelle had waited in her truck, there'd been a conversation between Josh, Justin and Evan that had resulted in Josh shoving at Evan, Justin looming over Josh, and all three of the men stomping away in long, angry-looking strides.

Josh had still been vibrating with the force of his anger when Annabelle met up with him in the parking lot of the Xxchange. She'd tried to get him to tell her what was going on, but he'd only shaken his head and grabbed her wrist, leading her into the club. Once inside, he'd ordered a shot of tequila then hit the dance floor with the leather-clad stud who'd watched Josh from the moment they'd entered the Xxchange. Annabelle wasn't sure leather-stud was the right type of guy for Joshie, but for now, he seemed to be unwinding on the dance floor with the guy, so she'd just keep an eye on him.

Movement from her left caught her attention. She looked over to find an attractive blond man leering at her. Too attractive to appeal to her, really, one of those flawlessly handsome men who could have been a model. Tall, nicely built, every strand of his highlighted blond hair in place and dark brows, and just perfect. Annabelle wanted to sling a few fresh cow patties at him.

"My name's Stone," the man said, offering his hand. "Would you like to dance?"

Annabelle gave Stone points for not tossing out some lame-ass pickup line, but as she shook his hand and introduced herself, she knew he wasn't someone she wanted to spend much time with. It was on the tip of her tongue to politely-ish decline his offer when she noticed the two men entering the club. Annabelle felt a fierce flare of heat spear through her as she pushed up from her chair and hooked her arm through Stone's.

"Sure, love to," Annabelle said as she looked up at him through her lashes. His answering smile showed off his perfect, even, brilliantly white teeth. Annabelle had to check her impulse to see if her reflection showed in his pearly whites.

Once they were pressed together on the dance floor, Annabelle discovered Stone was aptly named. His feet were certainly made of the stuff. She grimaced as he pulled her close and ground his dick against her belly. Her breasts were squished to the point they were nearly popping from the top of her dress. Annabelle grabbed Stone's biceps and tried to push away but he only tightened his arms around her hips and shoulders as he trounced on her toes.

"Do you think you could spare a centimetre of space between us?" Annabelle rasped out snarkily. "I'd like to breathe."

Stone's smiled widened but he loosened his hold. "Sorry. You're just so sexy, I want to feel you all over." He thrust his hips, his hard length rubbing against her.

Annabelle slid her hand down between them and squeezed his dick lightly before pushing his hips back. "Stabbing at me with this thing isn't going to get you what you want. Have some manners." She wanted to get laid…eventually, not right here on the damn dance floor. She sure didn't want to be dry-humped by a guy she wasn't even attracted to.

"Sorry," Stone said with enough insincerity in his voice that Annabelle's temper spiked. "But when you're wearing an outfit like that—"

Annabelle shoved his arms away and glared at Stone. "Oh for Christ's sake, you're a moron." She turned away, prepared to make a truly self-righteous exit, and promptly slammed into a broad chest. The big hands that landed on her hips sent a wave of lust straight to her pussy. Another set of hands, smaller but no less strong in their grip, settled right above the first set. Heat spread over her back as a leanly muscled body pressed up against her.

Sandwiched between two hard, hot bodies—and there were certainly two hard cocks attached to those bodies, each one nearly singeing her skin through her dress—Annabelle looked up and grinned at Justin. The lust in his amber eyes echoed inside her, and reverberated through to Evan's body behind her.

"Thought you boys would never get here," Annabelle teased as her heart pounded in her chest. She was a little scared, but damned if she'd let them know. With one hand clutching at Justin's hip, and the other behind her on Evan's, at least the two men couldn't tell her fingers were trembling. She hoped.

"Wasn't sure we were welcome," Justin said, his voice low and rough. "Josh didn't want us around you."

Annabelle caught Josh's eye and shook her head when he would have approached. "I'm not sure y'all are welcome," *or that this is a good idea, but...* "And I think Josh still doesn't want y'all around me, but that's my decision." She took a breath that threatened to stutter, then exhaled slowly as, careful of her wrist, she gingerly nudged at Evan to move around to her front. Once he did, Annabelle looked at the two men sombrely. They really were stunning, everything appealing to her, not the sheer perfection of Stone, but her idea of perfect masculine beauty. Annabelle nodded and took one of their hands in each of hers.

"All we're doing is dancing," she informed them. "If that isn't okay with the pair of you, then y'all best leave. I promised Joshie I wouldn't do anything without giving it some thought first." Her body would hate her for it, but she'd given her word, and she wouldn't break it just to scratch an itch.

Evan was the first to nod, then he glanced at Justin. "I'm good with dancing." He smiled at the other man when Justin only grunted. "It's not like either of us won't get laid at the end of the night."

Justin grinned finally and nodded as well. "True enough. *We* aren't the ones who — "

"Will be getting in my panties," Annabelle interrupted coolly. "I promised Joshie I'd think about it before I did anything with you two. I damn sure didn't promise him that about anyone else in this club." That knocked the smug look right off Justin's face. Annabelle figured she should have felt bad, but found it hard to when the truth was, no one else in the club held the least bit of appeal for her. And she *had* promised Josh, which meant Justin and Evan had it right, and that pissed her off.

Evan shifted his weight to his other leg as he glanced at Justin again, obviously sensing the other man's anger. As if Annabelle couldn't practically see the smoke rolling from Justin's ears. Evan opened his mouth to speak only to have Justin beat him to it.

"Well, Belle," Justin said, his grin slipping back in to place as he lightly teased his fingers down Annabelle's arm. "Guess we'll just have to make sure we entertain you enough that no one man here can give you what you need, right Evan?"

Annabelle rolled her eyes even as each man hooked an arm through hers. There was no way she wanted to let them know—especially Justin, with his smug attitude that she found sexy and challenging at the same time—that they'd already accomplished their goal. Not when she could have so much fun making them think they were still working for it.

Chapter Seven

Annabelle reined Slick to a halt and did a quick headcount on the cattle in the pasture. Assured each was present and healthy, she turned Slick around and let him have his lead. There wasn't any reason to rush back to the barn, and her mind had been drifting all week. Annabelle snorted. Drifting, her ass. More like plunging straight into the depths of the gutter. Her left wrist was healing up nicely, but her right forearm was sore, and there were two men to blame for that. Evan and Justin had made sure she'd kept her promise to Josh that night at the Xxchange, and Annabelle had been torn between throttling them both or dragging them off to a dimly lit corner to find some relief. It'd been days and every nerve ending in her body still screamed for something she was afraid to want.

But she couldn't stop thinking about it, dreaming about it even. Justin and Evan were both interesting, complex men, and sexier than they had a right to be. Most of their time together at the Xxchange had been relatively innocent—for that particular club, at least, which really just meant they'd kept their clothes on and hadn't come, though it'd been a near thing. It wasn't until the last dance before Josh had dragged her out of there that things had really gone from an ember of heat to damn near an inferno. Annabelle dismounted and led Slick into the barn. Her blood felt like it was boiling in her veins, and Annabelle stopped, Slick doing the same beside her. Just for a minute, it wouldn't hurt to remember —

Evan had more of the tease in him than Annabelle would have thought. He'd given her a searing heavy-lidded look as he'd pulled her close for a slow dance while Justin had sat watching from their table. As Evan held her close, one arm around her hips, his fingers teasing at the swell of her ass, his other arm draped around her shoulders, he'd leant down and whispered in her ear. Gaze locked with Justin's, Annabelle had drank in the filthy words Evan gave her, the vivid images he shared about what Justin would be doing to him later — and how much it'd turn both men on to have her watch.

Annabelle hadn't been able to look away from Justin, although what she saw was something other than the reality of the moment. No, Evan's hot words, Justin's smouldering stare, those fired the fantasy playing out in her head. Evan, wonderfully nude, bent over the side of the bed with Justin's thick cock buried deep in his ass. Evan described it in great detail, the way Justin's body would look, the ridged muscles, the sounds he made while he was fucking Evan, the way Justin's dick filled him thrust after thrust.

Annabelle's entire body had felt like it was on fire, the points of combustion — her pussy and the two hard nubs of her nipples — throbbing with each heartbeat. "And where would I fit into that scene?" Annabelle had asked, unsure of what she wanted to hear. She was afraid of what she wanted and how badly she wanted it.

Evan's smile had been wicked, his eyes intent, making her shiver with the dark promise in their depths. "You could fit in several ways," Evan had murmured the words against her ear, his moist breath causing her own to hitch. "Justin and I are both bi, do you know how many options that gives us?"

Annabelle's mind had spun with the possibilities, but the image Evan had fed her, the one of Justin pounding into Evan's ass, the two of them together, their grunts and words and ecstasy...

Tearing her gaze from Justin's, Annabelle had looked up at Evan through her lashes, noting the dark flush that was even then spreading up his neck. The feel of his dick pressed against her belly had made that part of her quiver deep inside, and she'd wondered if she could say no, if she'd even wanted to. She'd wondered how she couldn't say yes, when her body had burned for the promise in Evan's voice and in Justin's eyes.

"What if..." Annabelle's voice had trembled, which she'd thought it would never do. She had cleared her throat and forced herself to speak steadily, almost blandly. "What if I had been in that fantasy you just spun?"

Evan had chuckled, a dark, sensuous sound that had turned her inside out and made her press her hips against Evan, seeking some sort of relief. She'd nearly wept for joy when he'd slid his thigh between hers, giving her something to ride. The thin silk thong had been no barrier against Evan's lean, denim clad leg.

"I'd have been buried balls deep in your cunt," Evan had rasped, pressing his thigh more firmly against her needy pussy. "After I ate you until you screamed, tasted every inch of you. Fuck, the things we could do." Evan's shudder had transferred to Annabelle, and she'd had to use every bit of her willpower not to grind against his thigh and bring herself off. It wouldn't have taken more than that, Annabelle had known it, but she had already been dangerously close to

breaking her promise to Josh. An orgasm with Evan on the dance floor would certainly have blown that to smithereens.

"Or Justin and I would take you at the same time, each of us-"

"Annabelle, you gonna unsaddle and brush that poor sweaty horse out or stand there all day thinking about...whatever it is you women think about?"

"Damn it!" Annabelle started, glaring at Max. Her sudden jolt sent Slick into a minor tizzy, minor for him at least. Annabelle just managed to duck and miss getting her skull cracked when Slick slung his big head around, nickering his displeasure and threatening a nip.

"Are you trying to kill me, Max?"

Max snorted and took off his hat, rolling the brim with his fingers. "Been standing here watching you for ten minutes, staring off into space just waiting for Slick to knock you on your ass. Seems more like you're the one trying to do yourself some damage. Slick ain't ever been overly patient." Max eyed her for a moment then straightened his shoulders, his face pinching as if he'd tasted something nasty. "Look, if you need to talk about something...personal —"

Annabelle felt as horrified as Max looked at the prospect. "No!" Slick snorted and tossed his head again, prancing dangerously close to Annabelle's booted feet. "Cut it out, Slick," Annabelle soothed, keeping the anger she felt at her own carelessness out of her voice. She deserved to have her ass kicked for being such an idiot.

"I don't need to talk about anything," Annabelle murmured. She did, but the problem was there wasn't anyone she *could* talk to. The only one who might understand was Josh and he wasn't an impartial party. Rory wasn't an option, none of the men on the ranch were. They all had *a* partner, not *two* partners. Not that Evan and Justin were offering her anything more than a not-so-quick fuck, or fucks—Annabelle rubbed at her temple. This was entirely too confusing to think about right now.

Max came closer and patted her shoulder. Annabelle barely kept from squeaking in surprise; Max wasn't the touchy-feely kind of guy unless it came to Bo.

"Why don't you let me take care of Slick, you're looking kind of out of sorts," Max offered.

Annabelle swallowed the urge to laugh like a loon. *Out of sorts, indeed. Try confused as hell and so horny I'm afraid to walk 'cause I might just come in my jeans. And wouldn't* that *traumatise Max?* Annabelle shook her head. "No, Max. This is part of my job. I'll handle it."

"Well—"

"Max," Annabelle snapped, softly but firmly. "I said I'd take care of this. It'll piss me off if you think I'm some weak little woman who can't be trusted to do her job."

Max blanched and shook his head. "It ain't that. I mean, you do look out of sorts, but originally I came looking for you to tell you there's a man here asking for you."

Annabelle felt the heat spreading from her core, spearing to her extremities and making her a bit lightheaded. *Surely not*, she thought, Max only said *a* man. "Who?" she croaked, hoping Max couldn't see the way her nipples tightened and pressed against the plaid shirt she wore.

Max gave her a thoughtful look, as if something was clicking into place in his head. Annabelle averted her gaze, afraid he'd see more than she wanted him to. "Big ol' guy, Justin, said he was Josh's brother."

Annabelle grunted, feeling pole-axed. She hadn't told Justin or Evan where she worked, but it wouldn't have been hard to find out. She for damn sure hadn't expected either of them to show up here, especially since she hadn't called them and therefore hadn't spoken to them since the night they'd met. Which, in hindsight, she realised was the sure way to ensure Justin *did* show up here. The man really had enough ego for the entire male population.

"I'll be more than happy to send this guy off," Max offered. "Seems like a cocky, uh, bastard, if you ask me."

If you only knew. Annabelle did, if Evan's description of Justin's cock was accurate, well then, holy hell. She shook her head and offered the reins to Max. "He is a cocky bastard, but I can handle him. And I'd appreciate it if you would take care of Slick for me." Annabelle narrowed her eyes at Max as he reached for the reins. "As long as you understand that I *can* do this, I just *choose* to accept your help since I think it's best I deal with Justin." Hopefully she'd know how she was going to do that before she got to the bunkhouse.

Chapter Eight

She moved in such a sexual way, each step a promise whether she realised it or not. There was the slightest jostling of her breasts, and her hips glided smoothly, temptation incarnate. Justin's fingers tingled with the need to touch while he watched Annabelle as she neared the porch. As smooth as her gait was, she reminded him of a cat, taking her time to get where she was going, her body working in accord with the sensuality that seemed to pour from inside her. She'd get where she was going, and make a man — or men — damn glad of the wait as she did so.

The smile was slower in coming, but when Annabelle's lips tipped up, her midnight eyes gleaming as she swept his body with her gaze, Justin had to bite back a moan. *Patience*, Evan had advised, and Lord, wasn't that one thing Justin had never been accused of having more than a thimble-full of? It was a miracle he hadn't caved sooner and showed up on Annabelle's porch.

Annabelle stopped right at the first step and looked up at him, apparently not the least bit intimidated by the difference in their heights.

"Thought I told you I'd call once I had some time to think about things," she said in a lazy tone that stroked right over Justin's dick. Annabelle glanced at his package and smirked. The tip of her tongue peeked out and wet her full lips. Justin's hand trembled as he tried to keep from reaching for his dick, or for Annabelle. He wanted to do both so badly, he fisted his hands and propped them on his hips. If Annabelle wanted to look, he'd damn well give her something to look at. Canting his hips forward as he propped himself against the porch rail, Justin grinned as Annabelle sucked in a noisy breath.

"I don't like being strung along when I think you've already made up your mind," Justin told her. A woman wouldn't be looking at a man like he was every one of her favourite chocolates rolled into the perfect dessert if she didn't want what he was offering. Or what they were offering, as the case happened to be. She'd looked at Evan the same way at the Xxchange, and Justin had nearly come in his jeans as he'd watched his partner and their soon to be lover together.

Annabelle snorted and shook her head, though her eyes never went higher than his groin. "Just because I like what I see doesn't mean I'm going to jump into something like this without thinking it through. My body might be begging me to give in, but I *do* have a brain and that's what I use for making decisions." She looked up at him with that last bit and Justin didn't doubt the sincerity of the words or her expression.

Justin wavered between feeling victorious at Annabelle's admission about how much she wanted them and complete terror at the prospect of rejection her serious voice implied. He settled for remaining calm, at least on the outside. Inside, he was all raging hormones and abject fear. Whatever was building between Annabelle, Evan and himself was almost overwhelming in its intensity. Evan had been the one to admit it first, this clamouring need and borderline certainty that Annabelle could be the woman they'd both yearned for. Justin had agreed before Evan had finished speaking.

"Are you pouting or plotting some evil seduction scheme?"

Justin jerked at Annabelle's words, his mind snapping back into focus. "Neither. Just thinking about how you and Evan looked out on the dance floor."

"Ah, seduction, then." Annabelle laughed as she sprinted up the stairs, twisting as she passed him so that Justin felt nothing more a brush of air at her movement.

Justin turned to follow her, his eyes glued to the bobbing tail of her pale blonde braid and the way it tapped against the top of her ass. The braid was like a metronome, keeping time with the rhythmic movement of Annabelle's hips. He spoke without thought, staring at the mesmerising woman in front of him.

"I wasn't trying for seduction," Justin bit out roughly, his mouth and throat dry with a thirst no liquid would quench. "The two of you together were beautiful, light and dark, soft and hard, sweet and fierce. You have no idea how many times I've seen you and Evan dancing like that in my dreams." Justin stared at the toes of his boots for a second before deciding to spill the rest. "Hell, Annabelle, I see you two every time I close my eyes. That's all I was trying for, simple honesty."

* * * *

Annabelle felt warmth spreading through her chest. Unlike the other times since the night at the Xxchange, this wasn't so much a physical sensation as an emotional one. It wasn't her body heating up for Justin and Evan, and that scared the living daylights out of her.

"Well, I don't know about soft," Annabelle said, her defences kicking in. "There was a hell of a lot of *hard* involved. And as for sweet…"

Justin gave her a look that said he knew what she was doing, and this time, he'd let her get away with it. Annabelle had no illusions that he'd let her continue to deflect her feelings aside with a joke.

Grinning, Justin followed her inside. "I was referring to Evan when I said 'sweet'. I'd have to be blind to miss out on what a hard-ass you can be."

Even though that was the image Annabelle always tried to project, the evaluation stung. Annabelle rolled her shoulders as she walked into the living room. The tension only flowed from her shoulders to her arms with the move. It was only then she realised she'd hoped Justin would see beneath the tough-as-nails façade she wore like a second skin.

"So," Annabelle muttered, cringing when her voice cracked on the small word. She couldn't bring herself to meet Justin's gaze, not yet, when she hadn't had the time to bury her disappointment. "You wanted to talk, I take it. Have a seat. I don't know how much time we'll have before Max and Bo come home, though I think they're probably staying away to give us a chance to talk. Or maybe they're marvelling at the sheer novelty of me having a guy drop by, or—oh!"

How a man Justin's size could move so quietly was a puzzle to Annabelle, and one she couldn't be bothered to figure out as his strong arms came around her, pulling her back up against his chest. Heat rolled off Justin's body, encompassing her as surely as did his arms. Justin lowered his left arm down to her hips. His forearm spanned their width as his large hand gripped her right hip. Justin's next move was bolder, more like what Annabelle expected—and needed—from him.

He trailed his right hand up her stomach, then further up still, between her breasts. His fingertips teased at the quivering swells, his thumb brushing over one achingly hard nipple. Justin grunted as she hissed, then he cupped her left shoulder. A tightening of his arms had her pressed against his length. She felt him shift, his legs spreading as at the same time he tugged at her hips. Annabelle writhed, rubbing her ass against Justin's denim-clad dick.

"Oh, God," Annabelle panted, unable to pretend to be unaffected, not when every cell in her being felt hypersensitive and needy. She tipped her head back against Justin's broad shoulder, her hat tumbling to the floor.

"Yeah, honey, just like that," Justin crooned in her ear. "I don't know what I said that wound you up, but let it go. This is the only tension you need to be feeling." Annabelle shuddered as Justin ground his dick against her ass. She felt slick moisture between her legs as his tongue lapped at the skin below her ear, and she reached back to brace herself because her legs were suddenly too weak to hold her up. Grabbing onto Justin's thighs, Annabelle gave an answering grind of hips.

"Oh, fuck," Justin rasped, then Annabelle's world tilted and spun as Justin turned her around. She blinked once, her mouth opening to say something snarky, but Justin knew how to shut her up. The man was entirely too intuitive. He buried one hand in the hair at the base of Annabelle's neck, then his mouth crashed down on hers.

Annabelle bucked her hips and tried to press closer, her breasts aching, her pussy clenching, wet and needy for more Justin, more Evan, more everything. Her moan as Justin's tongue swept into her mouth—seeking out every sensitive spot—was one of pleasure and frustration. There were parts of her that needed Justin's touch desperately, but his hands remained where they were, one on her neck and the other on her hip.

Irritated and horny beyond belief, Annabelle nipped Justin's bottom lip hard enough to startle him. He jerked his head back even as he tightened his hold on her.

"What the fuck?" Justin muttered as he glared at her. "That felt like an angry bite, not an, I'm-horny-as-hell-and-need-you-now bite."

Annabelle clamped her hand down on Justin's thighs to keep from throttling the man as she glared right back at him. "That's because it *was* a pissed off bite *because* I'm horny as hell *and you won't fucking touch me like I need you to!*" Then Annabelle wanted to smack herself upside the head. She'd *meant* to say 'like I want you to', but the truth had burst free along with her temper. She shoved at Justin's legs, squirming as she tried to break free of his embrace.

"Annabelle—" Justin began, only to stop when the screen door squeaked open and was promptly slammed shut.

"I'm thinking Annabelle wants you to let go," Max snapped in a low, angry voice Annabelle had never heard before. She stopped trying to get free and twisted her head around to stare at Max and Bo standing only a few feet away.

"Might want to close your mouth, Annabelle," Bo advised. Annabelle did so with an audible snap. Bo turned his attention to Justin. "And I really think you ought to let her go, despite how horny she just said she was. A person's entitled to change their mind."

Annabelle felt her cheeks stinging as a fierce blush spread over her skin. Of course Bo and Max would have had to hear *that*. She glanced up at Justin only to see dark stripes on his cheeks, whether from embarrassment or anger, she wasn't certain. Justin kept his gaze locked with Max's although his words were for Annabelle.

"There's rules, Annabelle, that's how this works for us." He paused and Annabelle let that roll around in her head. Did he mean there were rules about what they could do, when it was just the two of them? Isn't that what he had to mean? Annabelle frowned and started to ask before she thought better of it. Now wasn't the time to let Max and Bo know what she was considering doing with Justin and Evan.

"Do you want me to let you go?" Justin asked, finally bringing his focus fully back to her.

No, not at all! "It'd probably be best"— Annabelle told him—"at least until I know more about these rules." The pending disappointment on Justin's face quickly shifted to a smug smile that made Annabelle want to slug him or fuck him in alternating waves. Both might work, even.

"You know," Bo's lilting voice was a forewarning for further embarrassment, Annabelle just knew it. "They make toys to take care of that problem. You can order them online if you don't want to go to Bob's Beat in town."

Max sounded like he was choking as he tried to chastise Bo. Justin snickered and slowly released Annabelle in minute increments, retaining contact between their bodies as long as possible. Annabelle just wanted to die and get the humiliation over with already.

"What?" Bo asked in a voice so innocent Annabelle had to roll her eyes. "Max? We've ordered stuff online, like that butt — umph —"

Annabelle stepped back despite her body's protest. She peered at Max and chuckled when she saw the headlock he had on Bo. Max had his other hand firmly slapped over Bo's mouth, and Bo's eyes were dancing with the deviltry his words had caused.

"You're just plain evil," Annabelle told Bo, shaking a finger at him. "Max needs to spank your ass until you learn some manners."

Max made another choking sound as Bo quit trying to get out of the headlock and turned a heated gaze on his partner.

"Someone needs to do the same to you," Justin whispered, and Annabelle felt her entire body flush with the promise in those dark words. "I'll pick you up for dinner with me and" — Justin stopped and darted a look at Max and Bo, who both seemed to be listening intently — "we'll discuss the rules so as to avert any more misunderstandings."

Annabelle nodded, unable to speak through the lust-tightened muscles in her throat. Her mouth was so dry she figured the saliva had turned to sand, the moisture seared away by Justin's touch, his words, and the memories of Evan's whispered intentions.

And damned if Justin didn't seem to know the effect he was having on her—him and Evan both were having on her. Annabelle found it hard to think of the one without the other, unless her mind was steeped in lust. She was tempted to tell Justin to fuck off just to see that smug look drop away, but she wanted what was being offered too bad to risk it. Instead, she settled for the meanest glare she could pull off and a few fierce words forced from her lips.

"Fine," Annabelle rasped, "but it won't be any more than talking." And she was going to hell for lying, no doubt, but her pride wouldn't let her bend any more than she already had.

Chapter Nine

Despite Justin's near-tantrum about it, Annabelle drove the hour to his and Evan's ranch rather than have Justin pick her up. She didn't want to be stranded there if she needed to leave, and being dependent on someone else for anything grated against her nerves, which were already ragged from her earlier argument with Josh. Even though she knew he had her best interests at heart, there were just too many things he didn't know about her for him to be able to make judgement calls for her. Too many things no one knew about her, except a few nameless people she'd experimented with during her one year away at college.

That had been one of her rules for quick hook-ups, the second a name was uttered, the whole thing was off. When she wanted anonymous sex, she wanted *anonymous* sex. The one guy who'd thought he had been smart by telling her his name had found himself on the floor, crying, cupping his bruised balls. Annabelle had forgotten his name before she'd walked out the door. Wasn't like the sex had been any kind of inspiration for remembering. It had probably been her disappointment more than whatever his name was breaking her rule that led to her knee getting up close and personal with his boys. Oh well, as far as she was concerned, if he hadn't bothered using his equipment right, he really hadn't deserved to have it.

Annabelle's amusement at the memory faded as she turned down the dusty drive. Her heart was slamming in her chest the closer she got to the ranch style house with its big front porch. Pecan trees provided a good amount of shade, and it looked like someone—Evan, she'd bet—took the time to do some landscaping. There were four garden beds, trimmed in a nice wood border, filled with colourful flowers. *How perfectly...domestic.* She wondered if Evan wore a 'Kiss the Cook' apron. And pearls.

"Bitch," Annabelle muttered. Evan didn't deserve to be a target of her snark, at least not yet. Time to tuck that down deep for a bit.

As she took the last turn in the drive, she saw the two reasons for her visit sitting on the porch. Side by side in the porch swing, with their arms over each other's shoulders, Justin and Evan were so appealing Annabelle was tempted to park her truck, get out, strip, and go at them. Luckily, she had a smidgen of self-control.

The men rose and walked over to greet her as she parked. Annabelle felt a trickle of sweat run down her spine, and her neck felt flushed, heat trailing up to her cheeks and down to her breasts. She wished to hell she'd taken a minute to check her appearance in the rearview before she turned off for their place. She probably had lipstick on her teeth and makeup smeared under her eyes. For some reason, that's where her mascara *always* ended up.

"Too late now," she huffed as she grabbed the door handle. And if Evan and Justin's expressions were anything to go by, she looked good enough to eat. That thought was entirely too appealing and left her feeling almost too breathless to mutter, "Oh Jesus, yes." She shoved the door open and arched a brow at the two hands extended to her.

"While I appreciate it, I've been getting in and out of vehicles for the past twenty or so years all on my own." So much for burying the snark, or maybe that was outright bitch. Annabelle wasn't the best judge of her moods. People tended to be too sensitive and get butt hurt when she'd only been trying to joke. She hadn't been joking just now. The truth was, if either of the two men touched her, she didn't trust herself not to jump him.

A glance at Justin's smirk and gleaming eyes told her he had a pretty good idea exactly why she'd said what she had. The man was entirely too much like a male version of herself. She'd have to keep on her toes around him. Evan, however, was frowning slightly, and his hand was still extended, although...there seemed to be a fine trembling going on there. His big eyes rounded slightly, a wounded look edging them. Annabelle felt a pinching in her chest. Surely that wasn't her heart? That damned thing was supposed to stay out of crap like this!

The pinch shot to her temple, becoming a pounding chorus of guilt in her head. *I can do this.* Annabelle grunted—she could only be so gracious, for heaven's sake—and placed her hand in Evan's. Justin's grin was triumphant, so she ignored it in favour of enjoying the way Evan's face lit up with pleasure.

* * * *

"Hard to resist those eyes, isn't it?"

Evan had to resist something himself. The temptation to smack Justin upside the head. He closed his hand around Annabelle's. Her skin was soft and cool despite the calluses that proved she worked hard for a living. Evan didn't mind them in the least. After...well, just after, he didn't ever want another lover who thought her only job was to sit around on her ass all day and look pretty. And be exhausted by it. Contrary to what he and Justin had been told, it could not possibly be that tiring to look attractive. Annabelle was proof enough of that. He and Justin had just been blinded by the need to find that one person who would make their lives complete, and who they could love and cherish in return.

"At least *he's* got something *irresistible*," Annabelle drawled, crossing her eyes at Justin. The teasing move took the sting from her words, mostly. Evan still figured it'd sting Justin's pride a bit, but his lover really did need to chill. Besides, he knew for a fact that Justin had quite a few irresistible qualities...okay, and parts, specifically a fat, nine-inch one. Just thinking about it had Evan clenching his ass, shivering at the dull pain that he loved feeling after he and Justin had a particularly vigorous round or two of fucking.

Justin must have figured out keeping his goading under wraps was in all of their best interests, because he merely nodded and gestured towards the house. "He has several irresistible qualities, and a very fine ass, too. But I can't ever say no when he gives me that look, and he knows it."

Evan was going to have to stand in front of the mirror and try to mimic that look. First he'd have to figure out what it was. Looping his arm through Annabelle's, Evan got them moving. Justin slowed down but didn't try to walk beside them; they'd discussed how to behave, and had agreed not to make Annabelle feel like they were going to maul her at any moment. Of course, the problem was, that's exactly what they wanted, and he thought, from the heated look Annabelle had given them before she got out of her truck, that she wanted it, too. *Way to go, dickhead. Now I've got a hard on that can be spotted a mile away. Talk to her!*

"So, how was the drive?"

* * * *

Justin tried not to snicker at Evan's attempts at conversation over dinner. He felt for his lover, he really did. Evan was so flustered, and so hard for Annabelle, he probably couldn't think straight. Justin knew the feeling, which was why he'd kept quiet for most of the evening. No way did he trust himself not to spew out something that would piss Annabelle off. If she left in a huff because he fucked up, Evan was going to be upset, and Justin wouldn't be happy either, but he really didn't want to do anything that hurt Evan. He'd been hurt so badly last time, his emotions more invested in their former lover than Justin's had been there at the end.

The guilt Justin felt over Evan's pain still ate at him. He'd known the relationship was failing, knew Mindy was using them and had suspected she was cheating on them. He'd been too wrapped up in trying to keep the ranch going, too exhausted from days that started at four a.m. and ended sixteen to eighteen hours later. His tunnel vision had hurt the one person he loved most, the only person who stood by him.

"Can I speak to you for a minute?"

Evan's voice was laced with a hint of anxiety that pulled Justin back to the present. One glance at his lover's expression and the barely cloaked irritation buried in it had Justin rising from his chair. Annabelle looked at him solemnly as they strode past her on their way into the kitchen.

"What's wrong?" Justin asked as soon as the door was closed behind them. "If you're having second thoughts, we can tell her—"

"Stop it!" Evan snapped. Justin stopped, stunned as he'd always been on the few occasions Evan had lost his temper over the years. "You're doing it again! It's not Annabelle, it's *you*!"

That accusation just hurt. "What do you mean, it's me? I haven't done anything! I've kept my mouth shut and let you take the lead—"

Evan stepped close, glaring right up into Justin's face. "No, you've withdrawn, just like you did the first time we brought Mindy over. It's like you're afraid to be yourself or something. And"—Evan took a breath while Justin tried to rein in his own temper, because, damn it, the truth *did* hurt—"you're not *letting* me spend time with Annabelle, *letting* me get to know her. You're *making* me do it because it's easier than you having to try." Evan stepped back and crossed his arms over his chest. There were no begging, puppy dog eyes now. Those brilliantly coloured orbs were shooting daggers straight at Justin's heart.

"You know what I think?" Evan didn't give Justin a chance to answer. "I think you don't want a woman in our relationship. Maybe you never did. Maybe you just knew how *I* felt and decided to humour me because, hey, it wasn't like I'd be having sex with another man, so —"

"Bullshit!" Justin snapped, his temper snapped, the tight binding holding back the hurt and fear that he'd kept bottled up spewed out Justin stalked Evan until the man was backed against the counter, his hands behind him to hold up his weight as he leaned away from Justin. "I've *never* lied to you! I never — God damn it!" Evan was right about some of those things, though. Justin's anger drained away as he hung his head, grinding his teeth as he tried to figure out what to say. The truth would probably be best.

"I won't say at first I wasn't a little leery," Justin confessed, remembering the way his own needs met and clashed with Evan's. He looked up and saw the fear in Evan's eyes, the trembling of his lower lip. The ache he felt at putting that look there, causing the uncertainty in his lover, threatened to tear Justin up inside. He groaned as he cupped Evan's cheek, wishing he had the words to tell the man how he felt, why he'd fucked things up when he'd only had the best of intentions. All he could do was stumble his way through it and hope Evan understood.

"I felt — still feel the same way as you. I *want* what you want, and not just because you want it, but yeah. You gotta know I'd do anything for you, give you anything. Please don't tell me that makes me a bad partner, baby," Justin pleaded, worried enough about the situation to not be shocked by the fact that he was begging. "But I never agreed to bringing in a woman just to keep you. I've just kept some of them I should have sent off because…because I couldn't stand to see you hurt when they left. Maybe I didn't want you to think what you're thinking now, that I never wanted a triad, and that was why I didn't tell Mindy to leave. I should have, though. I never should have let her in in the first place. I never trusted her, but you looked at her like that, and I couldn't tell you no."

Evan's lashes fluttered as he blinked away the moisture welling up in his eyes. He swiped at his cheek and shuddered. "So, does that mean you don't think Annabelle's right for us? Is that why you're not even trying to make us all...together? You're expecting her to pull a Mindy, or a Jane? Or that first one, Sheila—you think Annabelle will want to hook up with us just so she can go around bragging about bagging two hot guys?"

Justin didn't answer right away, giving Evan's questions serious consideration. In the past, he'd just let Evan have his way instead of listening to his instincts, and every failed relationship had hurt Evan more than it had him. Justin's greatest heartache was watching Evan suffer. Could he actually open himself up to Annabelle? She was a smart-mouthed, bossy woman who had no tolerance for puffed up egos and bullshit. She was also intelligent, caring and sexy as hell, and worth taking a chance on if Justin really wanted what he said he did.

"I think she could be right for us," Justin admitted, feeling a weight lift from his shoulders. Evan's smile was an added bonus that warmed Justin through and through. "We need to talk to her, though, and not this polite conversational shit. She needs to know what we want, what we expect, and we need to know the same from her. And"—this part was tougher to say, but he'd do it, not just for Evan, but for himself and hopefully, eventually, Annabelle—"I need to quit being a coward and keeping myself closed off, or hiding behind a smartass attitude."

Evan had this thing he did, it had captured Justin's heart from the moment he'd first spotted Evan years ago when they'd both been teens. It had been Homecoming, and before the game started, Justin had looked across the football field, his attention snagged by the best sound he'd ever heard. It sent tingles racing over his skin, and fired thoughts off in his head that he'd only just begun to face. He'd spotted the gorgeous kid several yards away, helmet tucked under one arm as he'd slapped at another kid's back. There was no other way to say it — Evan glowed when he was really happy, his cheeks tinting pink, his eyes sparkling. He lit up, and everything and everyone around him could do nothing but bask in that glow.

Evan turned that light on Justin now, and Justin felt his knees shake and his bones turn to jelly. He wondered, if Annabelle agreed, how he was going to be able to handle having two partners who could reduce him to a pile of quivering goo with just a smile. Annabelle would be able to do it, too, she may have some things in common with Justin, but she had that same effervescence about her —

"I think, maybe tonight, we should all spend some time seeing how we feel around each other," Evan whispered against Justin's lips. "See if we can be comfortable, get along, joke and tease like lovers do without someone getting pissed or mean. The serious talking can come later, once we've all had some time to get to know each other."

"And sex?" Justin didn't want to be an asshole, but he had to know. Besides, Evan wanted honesty.

Evan kissed him, a hard, deep, dominant kiss that rocked Justin to the soles of his feet. "Oh, that can happen as soon as everyone wants it to."

There was a tap at the kitchen door and then a creak as it was pushed open before either Justin or Evan could answer. Justin and Evan didn't flinch, or move away from each other, instead turning their heads to watch Annabelle slip into the room.

Annabelle clucked her tongue and shook her head. "Now really, I kind of thought y'all wanted this to be a three-fer, and here I find y'all slipping away into the kitchen to get all cosy without me." She dropped her gaze to her hand, studying her nails. Justin doubted she even saw them; he'd bet she was hiding her eyes from them, definitely him, to keep him from seeing any hint of what she was thinking. "A girl would think maybe she isn't really wanted. If that's the case, I'll be on my way."

Evan started to speak, but Justin brushed his thumb over Evan's lips and shook his head. "Let me," he mouthed. Evan nodded, smiling happily.

Releasing Evan and walking to Annabelle, Justin took her hand in his and, with his other hand, cupped her chin. He tipped her head back gently, wanting her to look at him. After the smallest hesitation, she did.

"That isn't the case at all," Justin informed her, already lowering his head, unable to resist those parted, pouty lips. "Evan was rightfully chewing my ass for being a standoffish dick." Annabelle's eyes shot wide open. Justin claimed her mouth, sliding his hand to the back of her head to hold her still as he bit at her lips, his tongue twining with hers, then dominating the kiss as Evan had done to him. Annabelle moaned into the kiss, her hands gripping his biceps, short, blunt nails digging into his skin.

"Oh my fucking God," Evan groaned behind him. "That's…damn!"

Annabelle sucked in his bottom lip, scraping it with her teeth as the kiss ended. She tipped her head to the side, peering around Justin. Justin simply held her tightly and turned them both so they could look at Evan.

"Does this mean we're done with the talking part of the evening?" Annabelle asked. She looked at Evan, who looked at him.

Justin shook his head. "I wouldn't say done with it, but I think the topics of conversation have just been changed. Belle, would you like to take this to our bedroom?"

Chapter Ten

The soft click of the bedroom door closing sent a trill of heat down Annabelle's spine. She tried to clear her head, think about how to gain back control of this situation, how to lead where she wanted this to go.

"I don't think so," Justin murmured, pulling his shirt off and dropping it on the floor. "I can see the gears turning, and whatever it is you're thinking, just stop."

Stop? Annabelle gaped at the man, ready to tell him who was in charge. A glimpse of movement pulled her gaze down. He popped the button on his jeans, then slowly unzipped them. Annabelle's pussy clenched, moisture drenching her panties as she saw the head of Justin's cock poking from the waistband of his black briefs. Her breath stuttered at the sight of it—dark plum in colour, plump and wide rimmed, the narrow slit beaded with pre-cum.

Justin backed up until the back of his legs touched the bed. "Evan, I don't think sweet and slow is gonna happen this time. Next time, maybe, or the time after that, or…" Justin trailed off as he bent over to pull off his boots.

Annabelle's head snapped up so fast her vision blurred. "*This* time? *Next* time or — who says there'll be another time?" Panic welled in her as she spun around to look at Evan. "This is just for tonight." *Isn't it?* Heart pounding, Annabelle couldn't decide what she wanted the answer to that to be, not even when a flash of hurt flickered over Evan's face. Evan, who she now realised was completely nude, his long, lean body bared to her. Like the flick of a switch, panic turned to lust. Annabelle clenched her thighs together, needing friction, pressure, *something* as she visually devoured the broad shoulders, the thin smattering of hair on Evan's chest, the dark chocolate nipples, the delineated abs that made her mouth water. She wanted to lick each ridge and valley, nip the hard swells of muscles. Her gaze dropped to his long cock, the cap stringed with dripping pre-cum. The urge to drop to her knees and suck that pulsing length to the back of her throat, cup the full balls in her hand, had Annabelle taking a step forward.

"Who says we'll need more than one night for all those times?" Evan asked, his voice lower and rougher than she'd ever heard it. "And Jus has it right" — he continued, bringing his hands up to frame her face — "no more thinking unless it's about how good what we're doing to you feels." Evan crushed his mouth to hers, his teeth scraping over her lower lip, tugging until she opened for him. His tongue plunged into her mouth, sweeping its depths, claiming every inch it touched.

Annabelle's eyelids slammed shut as she groaned, her tongue flicking against Evan's, battling for control. He pressed into her more firmly, demanding, taking, and Annabelle could only clutch at him, fisting her hands on his chest, then spasming before she dragged her nails over his nipples. The punishing kiss stirred her like a gentle one never would have. Every cell in her body throbbed. Her cunt grew wetter, her clit pulsed with each heartbeat. Slow, incinerating heat rolled up from her core, searing up her belly to her breasts, filling them with a need that made them feel fuller and almost too sensitive.

She was dimly aware of Justin holding her hips, guiding her backwards as Evan caressed her cheek, the rough pads of his fingers brushing over the pulse at her neck. Lower still, then her shirt was unbuttoned and the grip on her hips disappeared as Justin ran his hands over her sides before reaching up and tugging the now open shirt off her shoulders. A quick jerk on the material and the shirt slid down her arms and off.

Evan rumbled as he tilted his head and slanted his mouth for a better angle. Whatever resistance Annabelle might have left regarding the need to be in charge melted as the two pairs of hands stroked over her body, teasingly light caresses that left her chasing after them, twisting and writhing to get more, always more as Evan ate at her mouth, never once letting her find her equilibrium. The bright red lacy scrap of bra she wore was unfastened and pulled off, then her breasts were cupped, the heavy mounds squeezed as her nipples were rolled between merciless fingers.

"Oh God," Annabelle gasped when Evan finally lifted his lips from hers to trail stinging nips down her neck. He rumbled again and nudged her backwards.

"We've got you," Justin rasped in her ear, nibbling at the lobe. "Trust us, Belle, we'll keep you safe — or as safe as you really want to be."

* * * *

Evan struggled to keep the hurt at bay as Justin guided Annabelle to her back on the bed. He hadn't expected her protest that this would just be one night, but he should have. It had stung, then quickly turned into a full-blown ache that had sparked his anger. Why couldn't she see how good they would all be together? His pain had quickly morphed into the determination to show her just that. And Justin had called it right; letting Annabelle think and take control wouldn't have her seeing this as different from her other sexual encounters. Evan knew instinctively that she had always been the one in charge in the past. They needed to give her an experience unlike any she'd had before—and they would.

"Fucking beautiful," Justin rasped as he knelt on the bed beside Annabelle. He trailed his fingers over her stomach beforeinching up to her ribs. Evan took a moment to appreciate the contrast between Justin's dark, rough hands on Annabelle's milky smooth skin. He watched Justin cup the swells of her breasts, and his arousal flared brighter. Annabelle's breasts were mouth wateringly beautiful. Her deep pink nipples were already beaded, the very tips darker from Justin's plucking fingers. Evan knew how those fingers felt on him, the short nails scraping over his nubs, the way Justin pinched and twisted at Evan's nipples until he thought he would come just from that.

Justin cupped Annabelle's tits then pushed them together before rolling the tips between his thumb and forefinger. Evan's dick tapped at his lower belly at the sight of that, then his gaze shot up as Annabelle's kiss-swollen mouth dropped open on a moan, her eyes glimmering with need as her back arched, pressing her breasts into Justin's grasp. Oh yeah, he *knew* exactly how she felt.

Evan thought he might come just from watching, and that would not do at all. Dropping to his knees at the side of the bed, he quickly removed her boots and socks. Justin grunted his approval and reached down with one hand to unfasten her jeans.

"Lift your hips, baby," Justin crooned, and Annabelle, who Evan was sure would normally rip anyone's head off who called her baby, only moaned again and raised her ass up off the bed. Evan gripped the waistband of her jeans and caught the elastic band of some very skimpy, lacy red panties, and divested Annabelle of the last of her clothes. He skimmed his palms up her calves, over the inside of her knees, and further up to the soft, sweet skin of her inner thighs.

Unable to resist, Evan leant forward and sucked at one pale thigh even as his eyes feasted on her glistening wet pussy, the lips swollen with arousal the neatly trimmed pale blonde hair couldn't hide. He nibbled his way closer to that honeyed spot, inhaling deeply, pulling the scent of her musky hunger into his lungs. Her thighs trembled under Evan's touch and her pale skin was smattered with goose bumps.

Evan darted a glance at Justin who nodded at him before taking Annabelle's lips in an uncompromising kiss. Annabelle was making the sweetest sounds, throaty purrs that sent silky hot spears of desire through Evan.

Sliding his hands further up Annabelle's thighs, Evan pushed them, spreading her legs wider. He reached down and ringed each ankle, lifting them until Annabelle bent her legs and brought the backs of her heels to rest against her ass. Pride at her lack of inhibition, her ease at spreading herself for his viewing rippled through Evan. He greedily drank in the vision she made, her cunt lips opened now, her clit a hard tight knot peeking from its hood, and back down, her small pink hole, fluttering as he stared.

Evan wanted to dive in, taste and feel everything at once, lap at her juices and smear them on his cheeks and chin as he buried his face in her centre. Justin teased him about his proclivity for rubbing his face in his lover's genitals, but, weird fetish or not, and Evan said *not*, it was something he simply couldn't resist doing. Although he could and did understand that it might not be the best thing to do during their first time together.

His own hand shaking as his cock ached with the need for release, Evan stroked his fingers over the plump lips of Annabelle's cunt. Her hips jutted up at the touch, and the guttural sound she made had his dick leaking in steady pulses. Another soft brush of his fingers brought an even stronger reaction, Annabelle growling and trying to press into his touch. Her body quivered in a wave-like ripple as the scent of her arousal grew stronger. Evan gave in and leaned closer.

He sucked first on one slick fold and then the other, pulling hard with his mouth, knowing Annabelle was too far gone for anything softer. The salty sweet flesh swelled more as Evan suckled. His own moans joined Justin's and Annabelle's as he licked into her pussy, stiffening his tongue and fucking her with the stiff muscle.

Annabelle's cream was every bit the honeyed nectar Evan had known it would be. Her pants and gasps fuelled him to drive her higher. Evan slicked two fingers, running them through her juices, then plunged the slippery digits into Annabelle's cunt. Her throaty scream of pleasure was followed by her shoving her hips down, trying to sink more of his fingers into her. Evan began thrusting, short, hard strokes as Annabelle thrashed, her hips jerking, fucking his fingers. He reached an arm between her calf and thigh, planting a hand on her hip.

Firmly holding her down, Evan sucked her clit into his mouth, tapping it with his tongue. His fingers curled, brushing her G-spot, a ghost of a touch at first, firming as he carefully scraped his teeth over the nub he was suckling. A third finger slid in with the other two, and Annabelle gave a hoarse shout as her pussy rippled and convulsed around the thick digits. Evan pumped ruthlessly as he flicked his tongue rapidly over her clit, alternating fast and hard hits with slower, sucking pulls.

The bed dipped and he glanced up in time to see Justin scrambling off the bed. Annabelle tossed her head and reached down with jerky movements, burying her hands in Evan's hair. She was panting hard, loud skittery puffs of air, her eyes narrows slits of blue-black, her lips more swollen now, red patches of beard burn on her pale skin. Evan groaned against her clit, his fingers stalling when he saw the love bites Justin had left on her breasts and trailing down to her belly button.

Annabelle's hands tightened in his hair as she pushed his head down and thrust her hips up, demanding more. More pressure, more friction, more teeth, more tongue, more fingers, faster, harder, deeper—*more*. Evan gave it to her, moaning with his own need, wishing he could grab his cock and jerk. It wouldn't take more than a couple of strokes, he was so close.

"Keep eating her, baby," Justin rumbled, "I know you gotta be as hard as I am. Gonna fuck you till we both come — until we all come."

Evan's whimper of gratitude must have felt pretty damn good to Annabelle, because she slammed her hips up, shoving her clit against his teeth. Evan answered her demand with a controlled bite on the nub as he pressed against it with his tongue.

"Coming in," was all the warning Evan got before Justin spread his ass open and guided his thick cock to Evan's hole. Evan keened, arching his back as Justin gripped his hips and roared as he buried his steely length in Evan's ass. Annabelle bucked and thrashed, her movements jerky and her panting turning to cursing as her channel gripped Evan's fingers, holding them deep within her.

"OhmyfuckingGod!" Annabelle wailed, her shoulders coming up off the bed as Evan moved his fingers what little he could in her pussy's tight hold. He released Annabelle's clit from his mouth and rubbed it in hard tight strokes with his thumb, unable to suckle any more as Justin was pounding into him, fucking him so hard Evan knew he'd feel it for a week. He hoped he would.

Evan coaxed Annabelle's orgasm along, drawing it out until she screamed, unintelligible words, at least to Evan. He couldn't comprehend much past the blood roaring in his ears as Justin fisted his cock and drilled his ass. Evan gasped and felt his entire body seize up as cum sprayed from his dick even as Justin filled his ass with spunk.

As the roaring faded, Evan rested his cheek against Annabelle's thigh as Justin clung to him, his big body still shuddering. All in all, Evan thought, they hadn't done too bad — and the night was just beginning.

Chapter Eleven

Annabelle had almost got her breath back when Justin patted Evan's ass and tossed a condom on the bed.

"You two can start another round while I shower, if you want. I promise not to be long." With a wink Justin loped into the attached bathroom, his taut ass cheeks shifting with each stride.

"Shit, he's built," Annabelle muttered, thinking of how she had a soft spot here and there she just couldn't lose without the help of some lipo. Like that would ever be an option.

"Belle..." Evan's palms skimmed up her calves while his lips nuzzled the other. His voice skimmed her everywhere, setting flickering spikes of heat off in the most delicious way. "Can I fuck you now?"

Wondering what happened to the whole 'don't let her think' approach wasn't worth the time it'd waste, not when Evan was looking up at her through her spread legs, his sexy eyes filled with promises that made Annabelle's nipples draw up into tight, hard beads.

"I sure as hell wish someone would," Annabelle teased, batting her lashes as she spread her thighs wide. The sound Evan made, like someone had kicked him in the gut hard enough to knock the air out of his lungs, had Annabelle's cunt soaked. Keeping her gaze on Evan, she smoothed her hands over the mounds of her tits, pinching the nipples between her forefingers and thumbs. "But maybe you should watch and learn what I like first."

Twisting the hard buds, Annabelle bit her lower lip as she swallowed back a whimper. It always felt so fucking good, that mix of pleasure and pain. She arched her back and tugged the pinched nubs, adding a grind of her hips to the mix. Her pussy ached with each touch to her breasts, the pleasure zinging from the two spiked points straight to the inner walls of her cunt.

She felt more cream run from her slit into the crack of her ass and wondered if Justin would take her there the way he had taken Evan, ploughing into him with a force that caused her hole to flutter with anticipation. It'd hurt, but that would be part of the pleasure, wouldn't it? The idea excited her unbearably.

"Evan," Annabelle smiled even as she wiggled her hips, the hollow ache growing stronger. "Fuck me already."

Evan gave her a smile that sent a trill of fear through her. Not that she thought he would ever seriously hurt her, but something was shifting, the control slipping from her grasp as surely as Evan was rising to his feet.

"Sure thing, Belle, but first..." Evan lunged forward, grabbing and rolling Annabelle onto her belly. "Yeah, this is how I want you, so I can fuck you hard and deep, fast and dirty. That's what you want, isn't it Belle?"

"I—"

Evan sprawled over her, his body covering hers, the hair on his chest, legs and groin scraping over her skin in a way that only made her hornier. Evan's thick cock was wedged into the crack of her ass, and Annabelle couldn't stop herself from trying to push up against that tempting length.

"Imagine me, buried so deep inside your pussy you'll feel the beat of my pulse in my dick," Evan rasped, his lips and breath teasing the shell of her ear. "Justin's fat cock in your mouth, or maybe..." A hard thrust, Evan's hot length searing a path in her crease.

"Yeah, you'd like to feel Justin reaming your ass like he just did mine, wouldn't you Belle? And it feels even better than it looks. Justin's dick is so thick, and long enough to make you ache, and he can fuck an ass like no one else. Maybe a pussy, too, but I don't have one to judge him with, so..." He shrugged and ground down harder, repeating the move several times as Annabelle moaned and whimpered in a way she'd later deny.

"Evan, if you don't want to fuck me then at least let me get myself off." Annabelle was soaking the bed with her juices, the images Evan had painted for her so vivid she could almost feel the stretch and burn in her ass.

"You're gonna get off soon enough, Belle, just enjoy a little foreplay first."

"This isn't foreplay, it's torture," Annabelle protested as Evan continued the slow rock and glide between her cheeks. "My pussy aches, my—" She was *not* finishing that sentence.

So of course Evan did it for her. "Your ass aches, I know, Belle, but you aren't as ready for that as you think, not with Justin. Once he has your ass, you're going to know he owns it, and that'll be all there is to that."

Annabelle frowned. "What the hell are you talking about?"

Evan shifted to his side, his hand planted in the small of Annabelle's back to hold her still. "I'll explain it someday, but not right now. Right now I'm gonna give you what you've been begging for."

The sound of the condom package being opened kept Annabelle quiet. She wanted to feel Evan fucking her more than she wanted to make a snarky comment. "Come up on your hands and knees, facing the headboard, so Justin can join in when he gets done showering."

Annabelle tried to move with a grace belying the urgency pounding in her pussy. She peered over her shoulder, craning her neck uncomfortably so she could watch Evan. His twitching lips told her she wasn't overly successful. She decided not to worry about it and turned back to the headboard. Annabelle knelt and dropped to her elbows, thrusting her ass up and out, knowing it'd give Evan a good view of her slick slit as she spread her legs wider apart.

"You are soaked, and the sexiest fucking woman I have ever seen." The stark sincerity in Evan's voice did funny things to something in the vicinity of Annabelle's heart.

She put it down to heart burn and wiggled her hips. "So prove it to me. Fuck me like you mean it."

Evan snickered and thrust two fingers into her wet cunt, twisting the digits rapidly, pushing against her slick walls as he filled her with short, rapid strokes. "Sound like a bad porno, both of us."

"There are no bad pornos," Justin declared as he shut the bathroom door. "Just bad audio, and too many ugly guys. All gay men in those flicks should be hot."

As much as Annabelle would have liked to agree, Evan chose that moment to rub her G-spot. She gasped and arched her back, wanting more of that finger fuelled ecstasy.

"That's an unfuckingbelievably sexy sight."

Annabelle shivered at the change in Justin's voice, the teasing note gone as a deeper, richer sound took its place. "Been trying to get Evan to put that damned condom to good use for fifteen minutes," Annabelle griped, glaring at the evil man as best she could over her shoulder.

"Why don't you let me distract you from Evan's evil teasing ways?" Justin crawled onto the bed, sitting in front of Annabelle. He leant back against the headboard and sprawled his legs on either side of her. He reached for his dick, gripping the base and tipping it towards Annabelle. "You gonna suck this? Or would you rather watch me beat off while Evan fucks you?"

"Decisions, decisions," Annabelle teased, although she really didn't have an answer for that. "Your dick, you decide." Evan shoved another finger into her cunt, drawing a long, low moan from her.

Justin was reaching for her head, pulling her down 'til her lips brushed his pre-cum beaded crown. "Like any man's gonna choose jerking off over a blow job," Justin scoffed. "Open up and let me in, Belle. Wanna see your pretty lips stretched wide around this monster."

If it hadn't been a monster sized dick, Annabelle would have laughed, but Justin's big hand didn't quite close around the base of his shaft. Monster dick is exactly what it was, but she wanted to feel it in her. Parting her lips, Annabelle sucked the fat cap hard, her tongue immediately delving into the wide slit to pull out the pre-cum gathered there. Justin's thighs tensed, but he didn't moan. Annabelle really wanted to hear him calling her name in that husky voice.

Moving her arms, Annabelle grabbed Justin's thigh with her left hand and his balls with her right. His hips jerked only a fraction of an inch.

"You want it, Belle, you gotta work for it," Justin purred.

"Oh yeah, forgot to mention, Justin's usually got control that knows no bounds." Evan removed his fingers and grabbed Annabelle's hips. "Mine's not too bad, either." The only warning was the kiss of dick against her pussy then Evan thrust hard, burying his cock to the root in her trembling channel.

Annabelle cried out around Justin's cock, the sudden stuffing of her cunt what she'd needed so badly she felt the first ripple of her orgasm beginning. Tremors skated down her spine as Evan immediately began fucking her with long, thorough strokes. Justin tugged her hair, pulling her mouth lower down on his dick. Annabelle moaned as the walls of her passage convulsed, clutching at Evan's every withdrawal.

"Fuck, Belle, you're gonna kill me doing that," Evan rasped, plunging in impossibly deeper, harder, faster. Justin was fucking her mouth now, his hips popping, sending his dick into her throat. Annabelle forced her throat muscles to relax even as heat coiled and spilled over in her pussy, searing throughout her body as she came.

Evan grunted and slid a hand down to pinch her clit, sending Annabelle into a second orgasm before her first had fully ended. "Fuck fuck fuck! Belle...Jus...I can't hold back against this one."

Annabelle had muscles at both ends clenching, those in her throat around the tip of Justin's cock, and the ones trying to squeeze the cum out of Evan's dick.

"Just say when," Justin croaked, and that uneven, rattled voice sent another series of flutters through Annabelle. Evan added a twist as he pinched her clit, and Annabelle lost her mind, universes colliding behind her lids, as every nerve in her body pinged and burnt to ashes. Evan's shout of "Now!" followed a series of long, savage thrusts.

Annabelle felt the heat inside her pussy as Evan's spunk filled the condom. Justin's moan, that sound she'd wanted to hear so much, sent her channel back into happy spasms even as he emptied his load into her mouth. Annabelle moaned as well, the taste of Justin unlike any other man she'd sampled, salty, yes, but so sweet it overpowered the usual bitter tang of cum. She rolled each jet of the thick cream over her tongue, savouring it before she swallowed it down.

Once the last bit had been lapped up and Justin and Evan's dicks had both started to soften in her body, Annabelle felt a contentment so alien to her she didn't recognise it.

When she did, she couldn't get dressed and get out of there fast enough.

Chapter Twelve

"Belle—"

"Let her run," Justin hissed in Evan's ear. He tightened his grip on his lover's shoulder, holding him there on the bed. Evan tensed under his hand, and Justin couldn't help but notice Evan's own hands were clenched into tight, white knuckled fists.

Evan gave a jerk of his head, hardly even enough movement to be called a nod, but he quit trying to get up. Justin would have breathed a sigh of relief except he was too pissed. It took every ounce of control not to snatch Annabelle up and paddle her pert little ass until she learned some manners.

"Well, so." Annabelle frowned, her panties in one hand and a sock in another. "Ah, I really enjoyed it, but I have to go. Work and all, you know." Her frown turned up into a smile so fake Justin had to clamp down the growl that threatened to slip out.

Squeezing Evan's shoulder in a plea for him to remain silent, Justin pinned Annabelle with a look he knew from experience could make grown men piss their pants. "You don't need to bother coming back for more of this until you grow up. We'd rather have a woman in our bed, not someone who's too scared to hang around for a while and tries to run off like someone set her short hairs on fire. But we'll be here to listen if you want to talk." He really, *really* wanted to bust her ass when he caught the hitch in Evan's breath.

Annabelle's face turned bright red and she turned away, walking towards the door. "Yeah, well whatever you say, Justin. You obviously know everything," she muttered, but her slumped shoulders belied her blasé words.

Evan looked up at him, those big, wounded eyes pleading. Justin shook his head, doing some pleading of his own. Annabelle slipped out the door and, judging by how quickly the front door slammed, she must have run flat-out to get away from them.

"Jus, you can't seriously mean what you said," Evan said, his voice stretched as thin as Justin's nerves.

"I can and do, baby. She hurt you, and that's something I won't put up with. You've been hurt too much already." And Justin would feel the guilt for ages.

"She did," Evan admitted, "but she hurt you, too."

Justin shrugged a shoulder, suddenly unable to meet Evan's gaze. "Don't really know her well enough for that to happen."

"Oh bullshit. You're forgetting who you're talking to here. I see past that ball shrivelling glare to the man underneath —" Evan twisted and moved until he faced Justin fully. "I see *that* man clearly, and I love him to death, hon. He's such a good man, and he feels so much that it scares him."

Justin wished to hell Evan had *never* taken all those fucking psych courses. It was annoying to be analysed so thoroughly and accurately. "I love you like crazy, and that doesn't scare me at all."

"Sure it does," Evan argued, "but I am going to let you figure out the how part—that I can already see you're wanting to ask—all on your own. Bet you'll have it before I'm done in the shower."

Evan hopped up, a tremulous smile on his lips, and Justin knew *before* Evan got any further than that what he was talking about. Their earlier conversation. Justin thinking Evan might leave if they couldn't find a woman for them both.

Evan winked at him, although Justin thought Evan still seemed upset under the teasing façade. "See? You already have it figured out and I haven't even showered yet! You should get a reward." Evan batted his eyelashes, which made Justin snort in amusement.

"And what is the reward?" Justin hoped it was another round in Evan's ass. It would have been incredible to have a chance to fuck Annabelle's tight pussy, but nooooo, she had to up and run.

Evan fluttered his lashes again and propped out one hip. "Why, all of this," he said as he waved a hand at his own body. "And maybe even a snack after you finish munching on me."

Like Justin would ever be fool enough to say no to that.

* * * *

Evan knew Justin wasn't just trying to cheer him up, but himself as well. Still, he worried Annabelle might be done with them.

"So we just let her run." It wouldn't hurt to clarify that one more time.

"I'm telling you she won't run far. And think about this—" Justin stepped into the bathroom right behind Evan. "How many guys you think have chased after her?"

"Oh, probably all of them?"

"Probably," Justin agreed. "And she isn't with any of them, so I figure chasing her didn't do them much good. Won't help us out either."

"That makes sense," Evan agreed. He was a bit surprised Justin already got that figured out, too. Impressed and horny. "Now why don't you come on and fuck me?"

Chapter Thirteen

The bunkhouse was quiet. Bo and Max had been given the weekend off, a rare occurrence and one Annabelle didn't blame them for taking advantage of. The two men had packed a bag and hit the road as soon as they'd showered Friday. Annabelle didn't know where they were going, and when she'd asked, Max's cheeks had darkened and Bo had giggled, his eyes fairly glowing with happiness—and probably a bit of mischief. Wherever the two were, she hoped they were having fun. Annabelle grabbed a beer from the fridge, tossing the cap in the trash can as she plopped down in one of the chairs at the table. It had been a week since she'd walked out on Justin and Evan, and she'd expected... Snagging her cell off her hip, Annabelle checked the incoming calls. Then she checked her text inbox. Maybe it wasn't working, or she'd been on an area of the ranch where she didn't get any signal...

"Or maybe, just maybe, you really are a selfish bitch," Annabelle muttered. Justin hadn't said it that way but every time Annabelle re-ran that parting scene in her head, that's exactly how she felt. Evan had looked so hurt, and damn it, even Justin, with his tough exterior and that calm, reasonable voice he'd used — none of that had kept her from seeing the way his shoulders had tensed, the flickers of anger and pain in his expression before he'd covered it with a lay of stoicism so thick it seemed impenetrable.

And she'd run out of there, after the best sex of her life because…because why?

"Are you all right?"

Annabelle started so badly she tipped her beer over. Josh's quick reflexes saved her from a lapful of the cool liquid. "Thanks, Joshie."

Josh set the bottle down and waited, and Annabelle knew why — in this instance anyway. She'd fucked up here, too, practically ignoring Josh while she'd been in full subdued freak out mode. God forbid anyone discover she wasn't Superwoman, that she had questions and doubts about herself, fears and — she frowned and pointed at Josh.

"You have a big ol' hickey on your neck."

Josh scowled and slapped one hand over the purple mark while raising the other to point at Annabelle. "*You* don't get to hear about that, at least not right now. *You* didn't return my calls and only sent shitty little texts saying 'Sorry I missed ur call will call laterz' or 'Good here everything okay there?' *You* weren't willing to talk to me when I needed to talk to you, so *you* are gonna do the talking now."

Annabelle knew her eyes were the size of dinner plates and likely to pop right out of her head. And as shitty as she felt for pushing Josh away, she was also weirdly turned on by this display of…of *power* from a man she only now realised she'd secretly thought of as a pushover.

"Shut your mouth before you catch flies," Josh said, and the barest hint of a smile gave Annabelle hope that she hadn't fucked things up too badly between them. "I will even help you get started with whatever is eating at you. So, you fucked my brother and...and Evan last weekend."

Lifting the sweating bottle to her lips, Annabelle nodded, unable to look at Josh. She wasn't ashamed of the sex, but what came after still made her skin burn with embarrassment. Chugging the rest of the beer in a few short gulps didn't really help, getting drunk didn't help. She had a week full of hangovers to prove that. Pushing up from her chair, Annabelle tipped her bottle at Josh. "You want one?"

"No, I had more than enough last—" Josh stopped and cleared his throat, his gaze darting everywhere but at her. "Water would be great though."

Annabelle frowned, her eyes drawn back to that hickey. "What—"

"Nope. Not about me." Josh walked to the cabinets and pulled down two glasses. "And I doubt you need another beer. You've got bags under your eyes that I could pack for a six-month vacation"

"Thanks," Annabelle groused as she sat back in her chair. "Maybe it's a good thing your brother hasn't come hunting me down." She'd probably scare the beejeezus out of him.

Josh paused with his back to her as he stood by the sink. "Any why would you think Justin might hunt you down?"

It was easier with him not looking at her, or maybe a week's worth of regret made talking about it possible. Either way, Annabelle's eyes welled with tears as she stared at the battered table top. "Because after...after we'd all had sex, I freaked out a little and left. Fast."

Josh grunted and filled the glasses with tap water. "Did they do or say something to make you feel like you were in danger? Scare you? Or was it just having realised that there might be more to the three of you than fucking?"

"The last one," Annabelle whispered. "And I don't think...I've never done the whole relationship thing, and it was like being kicked in the gut by a horse. I swear something broke loose in me and I knew they wanted more than sex. *I* wanted more than sex. Somehow they managed to get under my skin, in here," she thumped her chest. "I've always been so careful, but they slipped right in and I ran. And now they probably hate me and I can't blame them."

Josh placed a glass in front of her then sat beside her. He took her hand in one of his and tipped her chin up with the other. "Why don't you do 'the whole relationship thing'?"

Annabelle managed to look at him even as her heart thudded in her chest. Her fight or flight was kicking in again, and she tensed her muscles against the need to get up and flee. That was what had led to this whole miserable week in the first place. And the answer was an easy one she'd been aware of ever since she could remember.

"Same reason as most people who avoid them, I reckon. Parent issues, watching my parent's marriage implode under my father's need to control every single thing my mother did or thought. Seeing the bruises on her face and arms when she didn't cave to him. Watching her pack and leave us there with that bastard!"

"She left you and Rory there? What kind of—" Josh squeezed her hand. "Did y'all ever hear from her after that?"

"No, she just…left. I looked for her, when I got to go away to college." Annabelle sat back, tugging her hand away from Josh's. "Couldn't find a trace of her, but she knew where we were."

"Annabelle?" Josh waited until she wiped her eyes, smudging tears she hadn't realised where spilling over. "Lots of people leave, whether it's by choice or not. My parents died when I was a kid. Justin wasn't much more than a kid himself. He could have sent me off to live with some relatives, or let me go into foster care, but he didn't. Justin gave up a chance for an education, a chance to be a kid, really, him and Evan both. They raised me and made sure I had a good home and got an education. Some people leave, but some people stay, too."

"I know that in my head, I do, but I think about how controlling my father was, how everything had to be his way—"

"And that doesn't sound a little bit familiar?" Josh asked, and Annabelle was so shocked by the revelation she couldn't do more than stare at him. "I'm not saying you're as bad as your father, you aren't a cruel person, but you do try to keep everything in your life just so. Anything that shakes that up sends you running."

"Fuck." Why hadn't she ever seen that? Had she chosen to emulate her father's stringent control rather than risk being a victim like her mother? It was simplified and something a child might see as the only two options available, and Annabelle had a sinking feeling that's exactly what she'd done.

"Your father's alone now, isn't he? Completely?"

"Yeah, he is," Annabelle admitted. "I get it, okay? If I keep being a controlling, uptight bitch I'm gonna end up alone and miserable."

Josh snorted. "I wouldn't put it like that, exactly, but yeah, pretty much."

"I don't know any other way to be, Joshie. I always thought I was being strong. I never realised..." And maybe she never would have if Josh hadn't cared enough to shove her into seeing it. "So what do I do?"

"Well," Josh scratched his chin and sighed. "I don't know the answer to that for sure, but I think part of it is like being addicted to something. Admitting you have a problem is the first step. After that, probably you need to start figuring out what you really want and if you're willing to bend to get it."

And that was the question she really needed to answer.. Was she strong enough to bend, or would she end up hurting all three of them if she couldn't let go of her need to keep her heart safe?

"I don't know what to do. I want..." *to be happy, to see Evan's eyes light up, see Justin burn as he lost himself in her.* "But a relationship with two people is hard enough. How can one with three work?"

"I don't know," Josh said as he shrugged. "I think if all of you want it bad enough, then you work together to build a strong relationship whether there's two people or a dozen."

"I don't even want to try to picture that," Annabelle muttered. "The dozen, I mean."

Josh laughed and the sound of it threatened to make Annabelle cry all over again. She'd almost lost him because she'd been too busy running from herself. She stood and went to her friend, hugging him so hard he grunted. "I really am so sorry I was an ass. You're an angel for putting up with me."

"You just want to know who gave me the hickey," Josh teased, but he hugged her back and pressed his forehead to hers. "Maybe I'll tell you the next time we go out. If you're very, very good."

"You tease! You're not even going to give me a clue, are you?"

Josh rocked his forehead against hers. "Nope. Not a single one. Besides, it's not as exciting as you'd think."

Like *that* statement wasn't going to drive her crazy with curiosity, but she'd wait. Josh didn't need a pushy woman prodding at him, he needed a friend — and so did she. "All right then, guess I have some thinking to do."

"Just don't go from thinking to brooding to sulking to-"

"I won't, I swear!" Annabelle patted Josh's back then moved back to her chair. "I'm turning over a new leaf and all that crap. And maybe you could help me, if you don't mind?"

Did she want Justin and Evan enough to risk opening herself up to the possibility of being hurt? And would they even give her another chance if she did?

"Of course, Annabelle, that's what friends are for."

"Please don't break into that song, I'm already teary eyed and that isn't going to help with the huge — thank you so much for pointing that out, Joshie — bags under my eyes." Annabelle poked at the swollen skin under her eyes and cringed. She definitely did not want to look in a mirror any time soon.

Josh shifted in his seat, crossing his arms over his chest and wiggling his hips. "So, what do you need me to do?"

"Just be patient with me, okay? And maybe tell me when I'm being a narrow-minded bitch. Remind me that I'm not always right, and that I want to...I want to stop being so afraid."

"I can so do that, but you have to take my calls or at least return them, Annabelle."

Cheeks stinging at the soft rebuke, Annabelle nodded. "I promise, I will."

Josh studied her for a long moment before giving her that sexy smile that she knew was going to rock another man's world someday. "And as an added bonus for repenting of your bad-friend ways, I'll reward you. Get comfortable while I tell you a little more about my brother. And Evan." He added the last two words almost like an afterthought.

Warmth suffused Annabelle and it startled her to realise it was happiness that was making her feel that way. Smiling her own killer smile, Annabelle propped her elbows on the table and her chin in her hands. "You're the best, Joshie."

Chapter Fourteen

Justin's least favourite chore was working on the books for the ranch. On days like today, he'd give his left nut to be able to afford an accountant. He scowled as the computer beeped at him, the numbers he'd just put in blinking. Squinting, he saw he'd hit the 'o' instead of '0'.

"Well, no fucking wonder it wouldn't take it." Backspacing to the offending letter, Justin promptly deleted it then re-entered it. "Damn it all!"

"Must be accounting day."

Justin looked up at his brother leaning against the doorframe. Josh was smirking and—Justin scowled again. "How big was that guy's mouth? Looks like he sucked on half your neck!"

Josh rolled his eyes as he waved away the question. "Adult here, remember?"

Justin pointed to the big hickey. "Yeah? Well that looks like something a horny teenager would be running around with."

"Like you've never sucked up a mark on Evan. Please."

"That's different. Me and Ev have been together for almost ten years," Justin was quick to point out. "And even so, I never put anything the size of a damn dessert plate on him." At least not where it showed.

Josh stepped into the room and sank down into the chair in front of Justin's desk. "So you want to talk about this hickey or do you want to hear what I have to say about Annabelle."

Justin's stomach dipped and quivered. In the week and a half since Annabelle had ran off in a panic, he'd started to call her several times. He and Evan had discussed how long they should wait before contacting Annabelle if they didn't hear from her first—or whether they should even bother. He considered calling Evan and having him join in on this conversation, but the truth was, Josh always clammed up around Justin's lover, or he became borderline combative. Neither of those would be particularly productive in this instance. Any instance, really.

"What about her?"

Josh shrugged. "Just that she and I are going to be at the Xxchange tonight. I thought maybe y'all might want to know."

Justin didn't want to even think about why Belle would be going out to the club. "Not really. She's made her opinion on me and Ev pretty clear."

Josh clucked his tongue. "I'd never have thought you'd give up so easy."

"She doesn't want us." And it hurt to admit it.

"I think she does," Josh disagreed. "She was a mess for the first week, and now she's trying to figure a few things out about herself. I thought it might be a good opportunity for y'all to remind her what she's missing."

Justin rubbed at his forehead as he closed his eyes. "Josh, it's not that simple. And it's not just me I have to watch out for. I don't want to see Evan hurt again, and I sure as hell don't want to be hurt. Annabelle could have called or even freaking emailed, but we haven't heard from her at all."

"Yeah, I know." Josh looked down at his hands for a long moment before sighing and looking back up at Justin. "I'm not going to betray her confidence, but I will tell you that sometimes people need a little push even if they're pointed in the right direction."

"What does that even mean?" Justin's head started pounding.

Leaning forward, Josh pinned Justin with a look. "It means that she's trying, but really, I'm not so sure you and Evan are."

"I'm not going to chase her. Neither is Evan."

"I'm not telling you to," Josh snapped. "I'm just telling you she is trying to figure things out…"

Knowing his concentration—which had been shoddy before this impromptu visit by Josh—was now thoroughly shot, Justin turned back to the computer and exited out of the accounting programme. He shoved the stack of bills into a sloppy pile then looked at his brother. "Why are you even here?"

Josh grinned. "Because I love you, and I know you and Evan don't play around on each other. I know y'all have always wanted…needed, rather, a woman to make you both feel complete. I think Annabelle's pretty damned amazing, and like I said, she's trying to work things out in her head. I think *she* thinks she has to fix some things about herself before she can contact you two. I don't know how long that'll take or how patient you are—not very, when it comes to anything else. And yeah, I didn't want her hooking up with the both of you, because she's the only friend I have, but you want her, and I know for a fact she wants—"

Justin's heart skipped a beat as he frowned at Josh, trying to figure out if that had been a deliberate information drop or just a way to hook Justin.

Josh bit his bottom lip as his cheeks tinted. "Whoops. Anyway, I just thought you might want to know we'll be hitting up the Xxchange around eleven tonight in case you want to show up."

Justin saw Evan appear in the doorway even as his lover spoke. "We'll be there, Josh. Thanks."

That firm tone Evan used brooked no argument, not that Justin disagreed. Enough was enough already, and the three of them needed to decide if they were going to try to build a relationship or not. "Yeah, we will."

"All right then." Josh stood and waved at Justin. "Guess I'll see you there." He turned and walked out of the room, muttering an 'excuse me' to Evan. Evan stared in the direction Josh had gone until Justin heard the front door shut.

"What the hell happened to his neck?" Evan asked, his brows drawn down low as he stalked across the room. "Did someone hurt him?"

Justin leant back in his chair and enjoyed the sexy picture his lover made. Despite not getting along with Josh, Evan was protective of him, and seeing him in protective mode sent heat coiling in Justin's balls. *Damn, the man is fine!*

"The little tease wouldn't tell me who put that hickey on him."

Evan's eyebrows popped up so fast Justin snickered. "That's what that was? Holy shit. You've never marked me like that."

"Can if you want me to." The idea of it sent that heat spreading up to fill Justin's dick. What had seemed tacky and immature in his opinion on Josh would just be fucking hot on Evan. And wouldn't Josh throw *that* in his face!

Evan hummed and trailed his fingers down his neck. "Maybe not right now, or..." Evan's slow, sexy smile had Justin shifting in his chair, trying to find a comfortable position. Evan unbuttoned his shirt and pulled it off, tossing it aside. "How about here?" He pinched at one little nipple, his eyes darkening as he worried the nubbin. "My chest, or maybe..." Evan dragged his hand down his muscled chest to the cut abs then further still. He skirted his package and brushed his hand over the inside of one taut denim clad thigh. "I bet it'd make me scream if you did it here..."

"We should..." *Talk about what might happen tonight, finish up the chores, fuck.*

Evan unbuckled his belt then unfastened his jeans. Before Justin could get his trembling legs to work, Evan had his pants and briefs shoved down and his hands braced on the edge of the desk, that pert perfect ass up in the air.

"Fuck first," Justin muttered. They'd both been too tired and disheartened to put as much effort into this part of their relationship since Annabelle walked out. It was about time they both remembered what it was like to love each other. "And as much as I'd love to take you just like that, I want you on your back right here." Justin patted the middle of the desk with one hand while he freed his cock with the other. Evan's sultry expression was pulling the pre-cum right out of Justin's dick. He thumbed the slit and shuddered as Evan sprawled out on the desk. His head dangled off the edge close to Justin's groin and, as tempting as the idea of fucking Evan's mouth was, Justin resisted. He couldn't, however, resist bending down and placing a sloppy, hot, upside down kiss on his lover's lips.

"Fuck," Evan rasped as Justin stood. He let his hard length rub against Evan's lips while he dug the lube out of a drawer. Justin hissed as his cockhead was laved then sucked the tip in the warm wet cavern of Evan's mouth.

"Nuh uh, baby," Justin mumbled, amazed he had the strength to not only say no but to step back as well. "Got other plans."

A few quick steps and Justin was between Evan's spread legs. He lifted them and made sure Evan had his feet securely hooked on the ledge of the desk, then Justin went straight for the sweet spot Evan had teased him with. He brushed his hands down Evan's inner thighs, his rough palms catching at the fine dark hairs smattered over Evan's skin.

"Fuck, Jus, feels so…" Evan shivered, the soft skin on his thighs prickling with goose bumps. "Oh, oh God—"

Justin nipped the inside of one thigh then the other. He scraped his teeth over a tasty spot on high on the right, where he could inhale and catch the musky scent of Evan, sweat and man and soap. Evan speared his hands through Justin's hair, holding him in place.

"Right there, please," Evan panted. His fingers clenched when Justin nipped, they pulled when he sucked, then Evan pressed into it and moaned.

Justin felt that moan in his balls, his dick, in every nerve in his body. He sucked harder, pulling as much of the tangy flesh into his mouth and as promised, Evan screamed, his hips jerking as one hand left Justin's hair to grip the base of his own cock.

"Fuck Jus, gonna come if you keep doing that."

"Can't have that." Justin nipped the now bruised spot then buried his nose in Evan's balls. He sucked and licked even as he popped the cap off and squirted some lube on his fingers. Evan was moaning almost continuously now, his sac drawing up as Justin worried the wrinkled skin between his teeth. He slid a finger past the tight ring of muscle, groaning when Evan's ass clamped the digit tight. Evan made a choking sound as he ground his butt down. Justin tapped Evan's gland lightly and was rewarded with a garbled sound that nearly pushed him right over the edge.

"Gonna have to get you ready faster," Justin muttered, aching so bad to be buried in Evan's silky ass that his stomach cramped. The second finger slipped in easily then shortly thereafter, the third did as well.

Evan was breathing hard enough to almost rattle the windows, and Justin couldn't wait any longer. He withdrew his fingers then slathered lube on his dick. With one hand on Evan's thigh and the other guiding him to Evan's hole, Justin struggled for a bit of control. Evan stole it from him by reaching down and pulling his legs up until his knees were almost beside his ears.

"God damn, baby, I hope you're ready."

Evan grunted and spread his legs even wider. "Yeah, Jus please—"

Justin pushed the tip of his dick passed Evan's tight ring then leant down, pinning Evan's legs between them, nearly folding the man in half. He grabbed the edge of the desk on either side of Evan's head then slammed his dick home. Evan's howl was nearly as loud as Justin's when his balls finally rested against Evan's ass. Evan squirmed and stuttered out "Move!" and so Justin did, fucking Evan hard, burying his cock as deep as possible with each penetration. Tendrils of heat wrapped around his dick as Evan's inner muscles contracted and rippled. His balls snugged up as tingling started in the base of his spine and spread to his extremities. Justin pounded Evan's ass like he hadn't been laid in years, and Evan begged for more. Everything Justin had he gave to the man until Evan screamed and his cock spewed stringy ropes of cum on his chest and stomach.

Seeing Evan come tore Justin's climax free and he roared as he pumped his spunk into Evan's ass. Evan's rectum squeezed Justin's dick like the silkiest, velvety glove and Justin shouted again as his dick spurted out one last blast. He shoved at Evan's legs then practically collapsed on the man.

"Feel better now?" Justin finally ground out. He felt like someone had just drained ninety-nine percent of his life force.

"Yeah," Evan agreed. "And we'll both feel even better after we get Belle back tonight."

Justin hoped that was the way it'd play out. If not, well, it didn't bear thinking of right now.

Chapter Fifteen

This was the last place she wanted to be. Annabelle thought, as she rubbed at the painfully tensed muscles at the back of her neck. "Only for you," she told Josh.

Josh grinned and rolled his eyes. "You only came because you want to check out who gave me the hickey."

"Not just the hickey," Annabelle said, "but *the* hickey. I mean, geez, Joshie, could it possibly be any bigger? Or darker? Or —"

"I don't want to find out if it can. It's too damn hot to wear turtle necks to work under my scrubs." He pulled open the door. "After you."

Annabelle stepped inside and grimaced. She really didn't want to be here, but the truth of the matter was she was worried about Josh. Whoever this man was, her friend was hooking up with had decided to mark Josh in a way that was almost impossible to hide. To her, it didn't say much for the mysterious lover that he hadn't given a shit about the difficulties his mark might present Josh. A small love bite in a place that could be hidden with ease was one thing, but this...

Josh grabbed her hand and pulled Annabelle to his side. He was bouncing on the balls of his feet, clearly excited as he tipped his head towards her. "Let's get a table."

The band broke into some screeching, throbbing racket that sent the pain in Annabelle's tense neck muscles spiralling in a thousand tiny shards into her head. Her stomach roiled as she let Josh pull her over to a table.

"I'll grab us a couple of beers." Josh flitted off to the bar before Annabelle could even tell him she didn't want a beer. Not with the headache coming on like it had. Josh disappeared into the crowd. Even if she yelled he wouldn't hear her, and chasing after him seemed impossible at this moment. Annabelle pulled out a chair and sat. She propped her elbows up on the table and dropped her head into her hands.

Closing her eyes against a particularly painful ice pick to the temple simulation in her head, Annabelle seriously questioned herself. What was she doing here? Was checking up on Josh's mystery man *really* the way to stop being so controlling? Or was she doing what a good friend does, and watching out to keep Josh safe? Maybe she was being paranoid about the damned mark; after all it was easy to get carried away when having sex.

The band seemed determined to blow out the speakers and everyone's eardrums tonight. Annabelle personally thought every one of the morons on stage should be publicly caned for aural assault. Once the 'song' ended, her ears were ringing so loudly she couldn't hear a thing. She risked opening her eyes just enough to see if Josh had returned.

"Are you okay?" Josh asked, frowning as he studied her. He set the two bottled beers on the table.

Annabelle pasted on a smile. "I'll be fine. Just a little headache. It'll pass."

"Oh." Josh's gaze flicked to a point over her shoulder before settling on her again. "We can leave if you don't feel well."

There was no way she was going to ruin their first night out together in weeks. "No, I'm good. Want to dance?" It'd probably make her head blow up, but the smile Josh gave her and the way his eyes lit up made it a worthwhile risk.

"Love to!" Josh took her hand when she stood. The band started up again and Annabelle let Josh lead her to the dance floor. How in the world was anyone supposed to dance to this crap?

Apparently by bouncing and humping any and everything, if the other people on the dance floor were anything to go by. Annabelle bit her cheek to distract herself from the pain hammering at her head. Josh did this little shimmying thing as he grinned at her.

"Oh really?" Annabelle shouted, doubting even then that he could hear her. She moved her hips in a rapidly increasing tempo, ignoring everything but the sort of rhythm of the music as she showed her friend how to move. She worked the shimmy up to her shoulders which set her breasts to jiggling in a way that might have been vulgar elsewhere. Josh laughed and shook his flat chest in response, and Annabelle couldn't help but laugh as well.

Josh responded by pulling her against him and grinding. He kept one arm around her hips and his other at his side, dancing in a manner that seemed sultry and relaxed. It probably was even sexy, although Annabelle had a hard time thinking of Josh like that. They danced and laughed through the band's set, and when the awful racket stopped, Annabelle realised her headache had faded.

"Thanks, Joshie, you don't know how much better you've made me feel."

Josh gave her a look of trepidation. "Maybe you shouldn't thank me yet."

And maybe she'd suffered a little brain damage with that headache. "What? I don't —"

Big hands gripped her shoulders from behind. Annabelle's heart did a triple somersault in her chest then tried to crawl up her throat. She was pulled back against a broad, muscular body and a thick, hard bulge prodded at her lower back. Annabelle gasped and glared at Josh as he nibbled on his lower lip.

"Hello, Belle," Justin purred in her ear and Annabelle's cunt slicked and soaked her panties, her nipples throbbed, and her ass clenched. She thought about trying to step away but Evan was suddenly in front of her, his hot eyes pinning her in place. Justin nuzzled the soft skin below her ear then nipped at the lobe. "Got tired of waiting for you to come to us." He ghosted a hand up her stomach. "So we figured you might need a little encouragement."

"I —"

Evan stepped right up against her just as Justin's hand ascended to cup her breast. Annabelle wasn't worried about anyone watching — hell, Justin kneading her breast was tame compared to the fucking and sucking going on in numerous places around the club. Evan's arms came around her, cupping her ass cheeks in a strong grip, the back of his hands rubbing against Justin.

"You want this, Belle?" Evan asked as he nipped at her other earlobe. "Want us to fuck you, drive you out of your mind?"

Two weeks' worth of hell seemed to lift off her shoulders, and wasn't that answer enough for her? Annabelle groaned and let her head fall back against Justin's shoulder. "Yes, please..."

Justin's chuckle didn't even irritate her. His warm breath felt so good against her skin, almost as good as his hands as he cupped her breasts. He pinched at her nipples with nimble fingers, doing it hard enough that she could really feel it though her bra. "We're gonna dance first, the three of us" — Justin promised — "gonna get you so fucking horny you beg me to fuck you." He slid his hands under her shirt, then under her bra. Her nipples were already taut and sensitive, and the first twist to the buds without any material in the way had Annabelle on the verge of begging immediately. Evan clutched her ass harder, then he was grinding against her, his rigid length rubbing against her stomach. He wedged a thigh between her legs and gave her something to rub her pussy against.

"Ride it, Belle. Rub that sweet pussy on me." Evan then took her lips in a breath-stealing kiss, plundering and eating away at her mouth. Justin had them all swaying as he continued to work Annabelle's nipples, his breath rasping in her ear.

One of Evan's hands smoothed down between them. He cupped Annabelle's pussy and rumbled his approval. "Already soaked through, I can feel your excitement here," he said as he squeezed her gently. Annabelle rutted into the touch, hungry for more. Justin rumbled and nipped at her neck, his hips thrusting, working his erection against her lower back.

"Oh God, please," Annabelle gasped as her nipples were twisted to the perfect point of pain and pleasure. Her entire body was tingling, her cunt and breasts aching for more as she grabbed at Evan's ass. "I can't...I need—"

"I know what you need," Justin muttered, then she was being half-carried from the dance floor, the two men who'd brought her body to its current needy state constantly touching her, touching her ass and tits, sliding their hands between her legs, keeping her stoked and burning for more. Justin stopped them right outside the club and tipped her head back for a kiss that demanded everything, his tongue ploughing into her mouth, seeking and finding every sensitive spot, his teeth scraping over her lips. Evan found the sensitive spot where her neck joined her shoulder and he bit and sucked. Annabelle's hips jerked, her pussy needing something, a touch, a tongue, a cock. Justin groaned into the kiss and reached down to pinch and rub at her swollen labia through her jeans, and Annabelle felt another gush of cream spill from her cunt.

"Hope you're voyeuristic," Justin rasped against her lips. Annabelle figured she was whatever would get either of the two men's dicks in her the soonest.

"Fuck me," Annabelle said as she palmed Justin's thick length. She'd seen it, tasted it, but damn, she had yet to feel Justin's magnificent cock inside her like she wanted.

"Oh I will," Justin murmured. He pulled Annabelle's hand away and tipped his head towards the parking lot. "Let's go."

Annabelle started to walk between the two men, both of whom looped an arm around her waist. She had a moment of clarity and stopped to glance over her shoulder at the club door. "I can't just leave Josh, I need to make sure he's okay with our night out being cut short."

"He's fine with it," Evan said. "He waved us on as we were stumbling out the door."

Annabelle had been too deeply into the two men with her to notice.

"Get in the back," Justin ordered as he hit the button on the fob to unlock the extended cab. He pulled open the door and tossed the keys to Evan. "You can drive."

Evan grinned and helped Annabelle into the truck. Her skin was prickling and her nerves were pinging; lust was a sweet roiling in her gut, spilling down to her cunt and spiralling up to her nipples. Justin climbed into the back seat with her, his hand already working the fastening on his jeans. Annabelle's mouth watered as he lowered the zipper and his fat, veiny cock bounced out.

"Let Justin sit in the middle," Evan suggested. "I'm less likely to have a wreck if I can see easier." He started the truck as Annabelle slid all the way over on the backseat. She unfastened her jeans and shoved her hand inside, moaning when her fingers rubbed over her clit. Justin narrowed his eyes at her as he shoved his jeans down.

"Evan?"

Annabelle watched with increasing desire as Evan tossed a condom to Justin.

"Strip," Justin said in that commanding voice, his hot gaze on Annabelle. Evan started the truck and pulled out of the parking lot as Annabelle shucked her clothes as quickly as she could. Justin's dick was a distraction, though she couldn't seem to look away from it. The wide cap glistening with pre-cum was like a siren's song to her. Annabelle whimpered and reached for the mouth-watering length, surprised when Justin didn't stop her.

"Suck it." Justin cupped the back of her head and pulled her down to his dick. "Open up and take it all."

Annabelle brushed her lips over the spongy top then darted her tongue out for a lick of the tangy liquid. Justin tightened his hold and thrust his hips, popping the head of his cock into Annabelle's mouth. Excitement burned through Annabelle as Justin held her head and began to fuck her mouth. The lack of control on her part was unbelievably erotic for her, as if in this one act, she could truly let go.

"Yeah, harder, with just a scrape of teeth right—ah! Fuck yes!" Justin fisted his hand in her hair and began burying his cock into her throat with each pump of his hips.

"You two are so fucking sexy," Evan groaned. "God, I can't wait to watch you fuck! Think I need to pull over so I can jack off while I watch."

"Sounds good, baby," Justin gritted out. "Better do it quick 'cause I gotta feel this"— Justin leaned to the side and slicked his fingers through Annabelle's wet folds—"around my dick now."

Annabelle hummed her agreement around the mouthful of cock and Justin let out a stuttered moan. He tugged at her hair, pulling her mouth off his dick, lowering his own head to bring his lips to hers. Annabelle squirmed as Justin mastered her mouth, even as his fingers teased the lips of her cunt. One long, thick finger slid into her aching hole and Annabelle gasped with the penetration. It wasn't enough, she needed more.

"I've got you, Belle." Justin tore the condom package open with his teeth then offered the pack to Annabelle. "Put it on me."

Annabelle sheathed his cock then straddled Justin's lap as Evan pulled the truck off down a dirt road. Justin held his dick in position with one hand and guided Annabelle with the other hand on her hip.

Annabelle parted the folds of her sex as she stared into Justin's eyes. "I'm gonna fuck you so hard you're gonna scream," she promised as she lowered herself down on his rod. Annabelle hissed as the crown pressed into her. Three moans filled the cab of the truck, and she slammed her bottom down, feeding her hungry pussy with one hard move.

"Jesus," Evan mumbled as he unbuckled. He bolted out of the truck and jerked open the rear driver's side door. Annabelle swivelled her hips, burying Justin's cock as deep inside her as possible. She caught a glimpse of Evan pulling his long dick out of his jeans, his hand fisting the hard shaft.

"Come here." Annabelle waited until Evan scrambled into the back seat. He sprawled beside Justin and she leant forward until she could wrap her hand around his. "Now."

Justin grunted as he smoothed his hands around her ass. He slid his fingers into her crack to tease the tips over her hole and Annabelle bucked, her ass clenching. Evan began stroking his dick as Annabelle started to raise her hips. She rode Justin's cock hard and fast, grinding down as she pumped Evan's length. Evan plucked at her nipples as he jacked himself off, his hand and hers moving so fast as to be a blur. Justin panted and gripped her ass tighter, rocking his hips as he fucked her.

Annabelle whimpered as she rode Justin, his thick cock spreading her, filling her over and over, the drag of him against the walls of her pussy felt so deliriously good Annabelle felt dizzy from it. She bounced harder, faster as Justin's fingers dipped lower, spreading her juices around. The tip of one finger prodded at her anus and Annabelle shivered.

"Yes, do it!" Annabelle screamed as the blunt digit pressed into her ass. Her pussy walls rippled and her clit seemed to swell. Evan pinched her nipple at the same time, and Annabelle thought she might just lose her mind. Spikes of white heat speared through her from her ass to her pussy, up to her tits and straight to the back of her eyelids where it exploded into a brilliant display. The burning and stretching of her ring sent her hurtling over the edge as Justin pushed another finger into her ass. Annabelle mewled as ecstasy filled her, breaking her down and reforming her in an instant. Everything in her contracted, her sheath, her ass, every muscle in her body as she slammed down on Justin's cock. Her hand tightened around Evan's shaft, and he cursed as hot cum spurted from his slit.

Justin buried his fingers in her hole as his other hand gripped her ass cheek bruisingly. His cock swelled inside her and he shouted as bursts of spunk filled the condom. Annabelle felt him jolt, his body quiver as his eyes widened in shock at the intensity of his climax. Justin shook and a tic started in his jaw as he seemed to melt into the seat.

"Fuck, fucking...hell," Justin rasped as he eased his fingers from Annabelle's ass. "Fucking gonna kill me." Justin pulled her to him, hugging her tightly even as he reached out a hand to Evan.

"Yeah," Annabelle said in what she hoped was a sexy purr but feared was a croak. She tangled her hand with Evan and Justin's. "But there ain't a better way to go."

Chapter Sixteen

"That was your friend Annabelle?"

Josh's heart stuttered at the deep voice coming from behind him. Sweat broke out above his top lip and on his brow. That deep voice had haunted him since the first time he'd heard it. The rough baritone seeped into him and settled right into his groin, filling his cock and sending tendrils of lightning to his balls. He nearly snorted at the way his cock thickened. Even when he heard that voice on the phone, his body reacted like that. It was some weird Pavlovian response to the unspoken promise of pleasure in that gravelly tone.

Twin bands of steel slipped around Josh's waist. He bit back a yelp as he was pulled up against a broad chest. The arms around him slid up until he was pinned with two thickly muscled forearms across his chest. Josh melted into the embrace; his body recognised these arms, this man, even though Josh had only felt his touch once before. *Nick. It's Nick.* He swallowed and let his head tip back onto the bigger man's shoulder.

"Jesus, Nick! You scared the crap out of me!" Josh waited until he thought he had his breathing under control. "Yeah, that was her." Though why the man asked was beyond Josh. His hopefully-soon-to-be lover had been very firm about his desire for secrecy. It'd almost killed Josh not to share anything about the mystery man with Annabelle. Josh tried to squirm around and get a better look at the handsome face he'd only glimpsed once before. He huffed in frustration as Nick's arms tightened around him, keeping Josh facing away.

A puff of warm breath ghosted over Josh's marked skin making him shiver. God, he'd let some guy he barely knew — didn't know — suck up dark bruises all over the side of his neck! For days now he'd been walking around brushing off questions about it. No way did he want to explain that he'd come to the club one night, angry at Annabelle's refusal to talk to him, and let some stranger do that to him. At least it hadn't gone any further than a heavy make-out session.

"Nick…"

"Hmm?" Nick's lips brushed the side of Josh's neck, nipping at the sensitive skin. Josh's questions scattered as he rolled his head aside, baring his neck in offering. Part of him was protesting the move, but Josh ignored that part as he felt lips and teeth and tongue close over his flesh. Nick's hands slid up to pluck at Josh's nipples through his shirt and Josh pressed into the touch, his body begging for more.

"Let me turn around," Josh pleaded as he groped for whatever part of Nick he could latch his hands onto. "Please."

Nick bit his earlobe then Josh was stumbling backwards, Nick's arms still around him as the other man half-carried Josh to a dimly lit area behind the stage. He stopped and spun Josh around once, then again brought Josh's back up against a wall. Josh caught a glimpse of pale blue eyes and darkly tanned skin in the seconds before Nick's mouth crashed down on his. Josh's lids dropped down as he clutched at Nick's shoulders. Nick's hands wedged behind Josh, cupping Josh's ass and squeezing hard.

One thickly muscled thigh wedged between Josh's. The hands on his ass tugged, encouraging Josh to grind his aching dick against Nick's thigh. Josh didn't need much encouragement. He moaned into the kiss and pressed against Nick everywhere he could manage. Nick's tongue and teeth plundered Josh's mouth, his lips soothing the stinging nips. Josh slid one hand down, his palm itching to feel Nick's erection. Nick grunted and caught Josh's wrist, tugging his hand away.

"Don't," Nick snapped. Josh's eyes flew open at the anger he heard in the man's voice. He found himself pinned by that icy blue stare. No matter how hard Josh looked, he couldn't see even a hint of arousal in those cold eyes. His mind snapped out of its lusty haze as what he *did* see finally registered. Disgust, and as if to emphasise Nick's feelings, his top lip was curled into a snarl. Josh jerked his hands back and tried to figure out what was going on as fear replaced the desire that had been building in him. He tried to escape but found himself held against the wall by the thigh spreading his legs and Nick's big hands holding his biceps in a bruising grip.

"What the fuck?" Josh cringed at the squeaked out question. His heart was pounding hard enough to make him dizzy, or maybe it was just terror at the sudden knowledge that he'd been played. He tore his gaze away and looked around for someone who could help him, but Nick had dragged him to a secluded area. Would anyone hear him if he screamed? Josh didn't think it would matter if he did. The music was loud, and screams weren't exactly uncommon given some of the sexcapades that went on in the club. Nick clamped his hand around Josh's chin and forced Josh to face him.

"She fucking *both* those assholes?" Nick growled. His hands tightened their hold, squeezing painfully. Josh's fear melted into fury.

"One of those *assholes* is my brother," Josh bit out, "and whether she is or isn't, or who she does or doesn't fuck, period, is *none* of your business, so get the fuck out of my face!"

Nick's expression blanked in the blink of an eye. It scared Josh more than anything else other than a direct threat could have. He bucked and squirmed, claiming each grunt and hiss from Nick as a small victory. When he brushed over Nick's erection, Josh's stomach clenched. Was the man turned on by the fight, or had he been hard all along? Josh didn't care to hang around long enough to ask. He drove a short, sharp punch into Nick's stomach then followed it up with a second hit immediately. Nick snarled and caught Josh's wrists and Josh soon found himself pinned back to the wall, his wrists held beside his head in Nick's big hands. Nick stepped forward and used his bigger body to hold Josh's still. Josh glared up at his captor and tried to cram his knee into the man's crotch.

"Now that's just bitchy," Nick muttered as he pressed harder against Josh. "Be still, I'm not gonna hurt you."

Josh snorted and glared harder. "Yeah, right. Because what? You don't think it hurts having you try to crush every bone in my wrists, maybe? Or having you use me as a buffer between you and the goddamned wall? Or" — Josh's voice hitched before he could stop it—"having you played me? You fucking looked at me like I was some...some..."

"And if I let you go, what are you gonna do?" Nick asked. "Run. And I can't let you do that just yet."

"Then we're at an impasse," Josh said. "I don't know what game you're playing, or why you're playing it, but if you think Annabelle would ever hook up with you, you're out of your mind."

Nick laughed and shook his head. "I'm not interested in her like that, I can assure you. And apparently one man ain't enough for her — "

Josh lost it. Nick's deceit, his sneering tone, his brute handling, all of it set off a fury in Josh he'd never felt before. Like a cornered wild animal, he turned into a savage creature, scared and hurt and pissed off. How he got his hands free was a mystery — he hadn't nearly the strength Nick had, but suddenly Josh was shoving and kicking, his fists finding tender spots and his knee finding the most tender place of all. As much as he'd have loved to stand there and gloat as Nick crashed to the floor, Josh's survival instinct propelled him into a full-out sprint for the club entrance. He shoved people out of his way, muttering apologies as he fled.

The drive home was a blur, and it wasn't until he was safely locked inside his apartment that Josh allowed himself the breakdown he'd held back.

* * * *

"Fuuuck," Nick gasped as he hit the floor. He'd seriously underestimated the little spitfire. One second of carelessness, of letting his guilt at his rough handling of Josh get to him, and Josh had jerked his hands free then proceeded to whip Nick's ass.

Nick sat on the floor cupping his bruised balls, shuddering as he heaved. He deserved the beatdown and more, he knew it. Josh would have been within his rights to kick Nick's head in. Damn it, he'd really fucked up. All he'd wanted was a little information about Annabelle and Rory, the half-siblings he'd never been allowed to meet—who hadn't, as far as he knew, been told of his existence.

Having seen Annabelle come in here with Josh a few weeks ago, he'd got this dumbass idea. Get close to Josh, pick his brain. He hadn't counted on actually being attracted to the cute little fucker. It wasn't like Nick was even gay, but touching the man, even kissing him, marking him, it hadn't been a hardship or the least bit distasteful. Then, tonight, the depth of his desire for Josh had shocked Nick.

"Fucking terrified me," he mumbled, feeling each beat of his heart in his aching balls. Nick had wanted to take Josh right there against the wall, and it had freaked him the hell out. Then there was the whole Annabelle thing—he wondered what Rory thought of that. Was he the over-protective big brother? Or did he not care what his sister did? How close were Rory and Annabelle? Nick's heart squeezed as he imagined them growing up together, squabbling and teasing each other mercilessly, but always, *always* having each other's back. It was a little fantasy he'd had hundreds of times when he'd been younger, except he'd been added to that mix, included and treated like he belonged. It would be nice to feel like he belonged somewhere.

Nick pushed himself up and slumped against the wall, his body stinging and his legs gelatinous. He couldn't bite back a grin. Josh was a fighter, and that had been a surprise. Nick didn't particularly care for getting his ass kicked, but damn, the smaller man had impressed him. Nick's grin faded as he replayed his behaviour in his mind. He'd scared the smaller man, hurt him, although that had been unintentional. Nick had truly only been trying to keep Josh with him. The idea of Josh hating him, of never seeing the man again had set off a panic in Nick, and he didn't understand it. He wasn't gay, he just wanted…he wanted…

"Fuck it." Nick stumbled through the club, images of Josh's expressions—adoring, lusty, angry, scared…hateful—all flicking through his head. Josh had been wrong about Nick being disgusted—or rather, he'd been right, but wrong about the reason. Nick had realised what a scumbag he was being, and how he'd fucked himself over by trying to manipulate Josh, *that's* what had disgusted Nick. Maybe he hadn't been too thrilled about Annabelle fucking two guys, either, but he could have adjusted. Instead, he'd been a complete and total ass, a bully, just like his father.

Ian Calhoun had ruled with the proverbial iron fist, keeping Nick and his mother under Ian's thumb. And apparently he'd tried to do the same to Rory and Annabelle and failed, because those two had been disinherited and disowned. Rory for being gay, and Annabelle for refusing to cut her brother out of her life. Everything about their father had been unbendable, and, although Nick was loathe to admit it even in his own mind, pretty much unlovable.

Nick sighed and rubbed at the back of his neck. Josh really should have just stomped his goddamned brains out.

Chapter Seventeen

Evan slapped at the alarm clock before the first note the obnoxious thing made was even halfway finished. He had a much better way to wake up his lovers. That thought chased away the last vestiges of exhaustion from the lack of sleep while also causing his dick to perk right up.

Surprised I can even get it up after all the fucking we did last night...and this morning. He and Justin had agreed ahead of time that whatever happened between the three of them, if Annabelle came home with them, it would be all about pleasuring Annabelle. They'd focused on her, filling her warm, silky cunt with tongues, fingers, cocks, until the three of them had been unable to do much more than snuggle together and pass out for a few hours.

And now Evan wanted nothing more than to be buried in Annabelle again. Reaching over Annabelle, Evan found Justin's cock already hard, wedged between the firm globes of Annabelle's ass. Evan ran a finger over Justin's rod and grinned when Justin woke, cursing softly as his hips shoved forward. Evan used that same finger and slid it between Annabelle's sex-plumped folds, cursing himself as the creamy warm flesh clamped around his teasing digit.

"Oh yeah, more…"

Evan glanced up to find Annabelle staring at him through barely-opened lids. Her cheeks were flushed with desire, her full lips dark and parted. She looked decadent and debauched and Evan had to have her.

"Get the lube and condoms," Justin rasped as he cupped Annabelle's breast. Evan tore his gaze from Annabelle to give Justin a questioning look. Justin nodded and licked Annabelle's neck from ear to shoulder. "It's what you want, isn't it, Belle?"

Annabelle didn't hesitate. She cupped the hand at her breast with her own and squeezed. "Yes, God yes, please. Hurry, Evan."

Evan let himself look at the image his two lovers made. Justin with his hair spikey and messy, his broad body pressed against Annabelle's smaller one. Annabelle looked deliciously tousled, definitely well-fucked, and the way she ground back against Justin, wiggling her butt against his groin made Evan want to dive right into to Justin and Annabelle both. *Soon, I'll have them soon.* He just didn't think it would ever be soon enough, not when he ached for both of them. Dragging his gaze away was difficult, because Justin being pressed against Annabelle's back like that was just hotter than hell, but staring wasn't going to get them what they all wanted. In short order, Evan got what they needed.. He tossed a condom to Justin. After sheathing himself Evan opened the lube while Justin lifted Annabelle's outer leg.

"Just raise it like this," Justin advised, his voice a thick purr that made Evan's ass clench. That voice always made him spread his legs or drop down on all fours instantly, but right now he had something else in mind. Coating his fingers liberally with the viscous liquid, Evan watched Justin pluck at Annabelle's nipples. The buds were tight and swollen, the skin red and abraded, and Annabelle was loving every minute of it, her hips rocking against Justin's groin as she shoved her chest forward in a demand for more. Evan waited until she whimpered then he thrust two fingers into her pussy. The tight grip on his digits made Evan's eyes cross. He couldn't wait to be in that velvety vice.

"God, Evan, Justin, I need you!" Annabelle thrashed and writhed, and Evan had no doubt she was fully awake now. Justin locked his arm around Annabelle's waist and rolled to his back, taking Annabelle with him so that she lay on her back on top of him.

Evan moved as well, settling on his knees between his lovers' spread legs. He locked stares with Annabelle and asked, "Are you sure you're ready for this?"

"Are you fucking kidding?" Annabelle's snarl was laced with so much frustration Evan almost snickered. Okay, so she was awake and aware, and aching. *Got it.*

Justin now had both hands on Annabelle's tits, his thumbs and forefingers pinching and plucking. Evan grabbed the base of Justin's cock and held it in position. Annabelle shifted position, still keeping her back to Justin, sitting up and straddling his groin. She sank down, enveloping Justin's dick fully in one smooth glide. Evan was riveted by the sight of Justin's body joined with Annabelle's. Their moans inflamed Evan's own need, causing a throbbing ache in his balls. Annabelle rode Justin slowly for a minute, her lashes fluttering as she sighed, sounding so content it made Evan's heart swell nearly as much as his dick. Then she stopped, only to rise up and reposition herself until she was once again astride Justin's cock, this time facing him. She glanced back over her shoulder at Evan, arched a brow, then turned back to face Justin as she lowered herself on top of him.

"Come here," Annabelle ordered, arching her back like a cat being stroked. "I need you, Evan."

Evan's lungs constricted, pushing his breath out in a *whoosh*. He wanted this…them, so bad it hurt. The fact that Annabelle hadn't run off made him feel light inside, as if his blood was saturated in helium, and it ratcheted up his desire to a level he hadn't often felt.

Scooting closer, he carefully lined his dick up to Annabelle's stuffed pussy. Annabelle purred as Justin rolled his hips deep into the mattress. When only the tip of Justin's shaft remained inside those constricting walls, Evan lined his dick up with Justin's and fisted them both as best he could. Slowly, in minute increments that threatened to fry Evan's brain, the two men worked their lengths into Annabelle's sleek passage.

A long, guttural groan tore free from Annabelle as Evan and Justin rocked into her. Evan hooked his hands around the top of her thighs and, on an unspoken cue, he and Justin thrust and seated themselves as deeply inside their Belle as they could.

Evan wanted to take a moment to study and imprint every detail of this event into his memories. He tried to absorb everything, but Annabelle made another one of those needy whimpering sounds that drove him wild.

"We've got you, baby," Evan promised, then he tightened his grip on Annabelle's thighs and began a slow series of thrusts. He couldn't talk, couldn't think, not with Justin's cock rubbing against his, not with Annabelle's inner muscles clenching and rippling, nearly pulling the cum right out of him. All he could do was what he wanted to do, and he was doing it right now. Evan increased the speed and force of his thrusts even though he wanted this to last for eternity. Justin's cockhead was rubbing Evan just right, and the hot, silky feel of Annabelle's sweet pussy was shattering Evan's control. Needing Annabelle to come first, he slid a hand down, relishing the smooth sweat slicked skin and the neatly trimmed pale white pubic hair. His fingers brushed over Annabelle's swollen clit and Annabelle bucked and shouted, her eyes shooting wide open.

"Yeah, Belle, fuckin' hell," Justin panted, his fingers working Annabelle's nipples as his short jerky thrusts became harder and frantic. "Ev, Ev, baby…"

Yeah, Evan needed it too. His balls were drawn up so tight he thought they might have crawled up inside him, his thighs were quivering, and his stomach ached as a firestorm exploded inside him. His fingers pinched Annabelle's pearl and Annabelle screamed, her whole body going taut as strung barbed wire.

Evan shoved his dick in deep as he roared his release, unable to move any more in the tight vice of Annabelle's body. Justin's gasped "Fuck fuck fuck!" morphed into a strangled yell as Annabelle's cunt squeezed and massaged their dicks, and Evan could only grunt as his vision dimmed and his head spun. Somehow, he managed to withdraw from Annabelle's body before collapsing backwards on the bed. It took the rest of his energy to crawl beside Annabelle, cocooning her between himself and Justin once again.

"Belle, we still have to talk," Justin said, breaking the comfortable silence they'd been sharing. Evan felt

Annabelle tense beside him and knew Justin felt it, too. Before he could get paranoid, Annabelle was pushing herself up until her back was braced against the headboard.

"We do," Annabelle agreed, her midnight eyes showing none of the panic Evan had feared would be there. "But I didn't run, and I'm not planning to, but we have got to figure out what's going on between the three of us. Is it casual, convenience or what? Only..." Annabelle glanced at the alarm clock. "I have to work, y'all ought to understand that. Why don't we agree to have dinner together tonight, and maybe after we eat, we can all get this figured out."

Evan was pretty sure he and Justin had it figured out, but he'd be damned if he was going to tell Annabelle she didn't have a chance of resisting them. What was growing between the three of them was getting stronger with each beat of Evan's heart. Still, he couldn't point that out just yet.

After he and Justin agreed, Annabelle patted both their asses. "All right, then. We will talk about everything you want to tonight. Now, I really do need to get ready."

Evan nodded and rolled away until he was sitting on the edge of the bed. He watched as Annabelle began gathering her clothes. From her jeans she pulled out a cell phone then gasped, turning slightly green.

"What's wrong?" Evan asked as he and Justin both moved to her sides.

Annabelle looked stricken and confused. "It's...I think my dad tried to call, and that scares me."

140

Chapter Eighteen

"You want to call him back?"

Annabelle shook her head in answer to Justin's question and tossed the phone back onto her jeans. "No. He called a little after four in the morning, the usual time he calls drunk and tries to keep me from hanging up on him."

"Why would you hang up on your dad?" Evan asked, and Annabelle had a very clear image of her future if she decided to try to forge on with these two men. She'd be hounded relentlessly any time Justin or Evan thought there was cause for it, and damn it all, why did that actually make her feel all warm and tingly inside?

"Because he a vicious, abusive, manipulative, bigoted—"

"Ah," Justin cut in, "one of those. Guess you'll never be taking us home to meet the folks, huh?"

Although the question was asked in jest, Annabelle could hear the underlying vulnerability, the tremor of desire to be more than just fuck buddies in Justin's voice. She glanced at him, unsurprised to find him looking down at a spot on the sheet. God only knew what was on the sheet, there'd been body fluids all over the three of them. Evan, however, was meeting her head on, his bright eyes gleaming in a way that kind of frightened her. *He* wasn't trying to pass anything off as a joke, that look said, even as it warned her not to hurt Justin.

"It's only my dad," Annabelle finally answered, "and no, I'm not welcome there as long as I have anything to do with Rory since he's gay. It's a safe bet I'll never sit at the dinner table with my father again. There's no way he'd welcome either of you or Josh or me if I was with y'all, so no to dinner with him."

Annabelle hoped it was enough of a declaration, because she really couldn't commit to more, not when she didn't know where she stood with Justin and Evan, and not—although yeah, she was a grown woman—without Rory's approval. She'd already lost her father, or he'd lost her, whatever. She didn't want to lose Rory as well, and she wasn't real sure he'd handle his sister being part of a ménage very well. He was kind of a prude.

When she dared to look at Justin again, the sweet smile on his lips caused a gush of warm, thick moisture to leak from her cunt. Evan was wearing a matching smile and it sent flickers of need rolling through her in waves. "What? Why're y'all looking at me like that?"

"Was that your way of saying you'll give us a shot?" Evan asked. "Or am I reading more into the whole 'no dinner with dad 'cause he won't accept me and Justin' than I should have?"

Feeling shy and timid wasn't something Annabelle was used to, and she quashed both emotions before they could take root. "Yeah, that's actually what I meant. Figured you two were smart enough to figure it out, but apparently..." Annabelle rolled her eyes then squealed when she was tackled by the two sexy men who'd somehow managed to sneak under her skin.

"That's good enough," Justin purred in her ear, pausing to nibble on the sensitive shell. "For now, at least."

Annabelle's witty retort was cut short by Evan's talented lips latching on to her clit. That beat getting the last word any day.

* * * *

Josh was definitely paranoid. After having a nice little meltdown once he'd reached his place, shedding a few tears and cursing his miserable luck with men, he'd stood at the window and stared out at the crappy neighbourhood he lived in. Three times he'd seen a big Dodge 2500 cruise by his place, and though he couldn't make out the plates, he could see well enough to know they weren't Texas plates tacked onto the monstrous truck. Of course, that could just mean whoever had been cruising by was lost, and Josh had put it down to just that when he'd finally given in to exhaustion and slept.

But now, here he sat at the diner across from the hospital, and unless he was flat out crazy, the same truck that'd been cruising by his apartment last night had just driven by twice in a matter of minutes, and of course the damned windows were tinted so dark Josh couldn't see who was driving.

Of course, because if he was going to have a stalker, it only stood to reason that he wouldn't know who the fuck the psycho was. That'd make it way too easy to get a restraining order, wouldn't it?

Josh pulled out his cell phone and fired off another text to Annabelle. He didn't know what she was doing…well, knowing his horny brother and his equally horny partner, Josh probably *did* know what she was doing, and that was just…not something he ever, *ever* needed to think about again. Still, he wished the three of them would quit screwing around long enough for Annabelle to give him a call. He was a little bit of a mess just now.

And there went the truck again. Josh generally liked those big old Dodges, especially the black ones loaded with chrome like the one his stalker was driving, but if this continued, he might have to make Chevy his favourite truck manufacturer. This time he grabbed his phone and snapped a quick picture, just in case. If he went missing or anything like that, maybe the cops would have a place to start.

Josh sent the picture off to Annabelle, along with the text telling her he thought whoever was driving that truck might be following him, then he shoved his plate aside, his appetite gone. Maybe he really was just being paranoid; it wasn't like they lived in a booming metropolis. There was a good chance it was all a coincidence, really.

He tossed a tip on the table then edged out of the booth, ignoring the occasional sneer sent his way from people who didn't like his hot pink scrubs. Or maybe they didn't like penguins, which Josh absolutely loved along with the bright pink, which made these his absolute favourite scrubs.

Seriously, there were no cooler scrubs in existence. And if it wasn't the scrubs, if those dipshits had a problem with the way Josh swished a bit when he walked—well, he usually didn't swish much at all, but if inbred bigots wanted to glare, he'd give 'em a show—then screw them all. Josh wasn't stepping in a closet for anyone. These hicks could take their delicate sensibilities and cram 'em—

"Wow, vicious bitch today or what?" Josh mumbled as he waited at the register for his bill. *Definitely need to rein in the desire to kick in the natives' teeth.* His knuckles were scraped and raw from beating the crap out of Nick last night. Josh grinned at the memory even as his heart contracted painfully. *At least I didn't hurt my kneecap. So much easier being the racker rather than the rackee.*

Josh paid his bill then left the diner. As he waited to jog across the street and return to work, his skin prickled as a sense of unease rushed up his spine. Josh looked around as he rubbed at the back of his neck. Nothing seemed out of the ordinary, no ominous black Dodges, no sign waving haters, no scowling homophobes...well, besides the dude glaring at him from across the street.

Josh wasn't a hundred per cent sure the man was glaring, since the brim of a black Stetson shaded his eyes, but it sure as hell *felt* like he was glaring. Josh was definitely picking up angry vibes from someone. Tall, dark and hateful seemed the most likely candidate.

His phone rang just as Josh started to cross the street. Plucking the cell from his pocket, Josh kept one eye on the approaching man in the black hat as he stepped onto the crosswalk. After punching the answer icon, Josh put the phone to his ear, hoping it was Annabelle. He hadn't wanted to take his gaze off the possibly threatening form coming his way long enough to check the caller ID.

"Hello?"

"Hey Josh," Rory's deep voice rumbled over the line. Josh was so startled he tripped and nearly face planted the asphalt. A strong hand clamped around his biceps jerked him upright. Before Josh could even thank his rescuer, the man and his hand were gone. Josh risked a peek over his shoulder and nearly stumbled again when he realised his supposed hateful cowboy had actually been the one who'd kept him from falling.

"Maybe he wants to keep me alive so he can kill me himself," Josh mused.

"What?" Rory snapped. "Josh, are you drunk or something?"

Josh laughed. He'd forgotten Rory was even on the phone. Josh had been too distracted by his rescuer's very fine, very tempting tight ass as he'd walked away. "No, not drunk, just thinking out loud. Sorry. What'd you need, Rory?" Josh wasn't dumb, Rory had never called him before, although he had Josh's number. So did Chance, and Max, and Bo, and Josh had theirs as well.

Rory whispered something to someone else, probably Chance, Josh thought. Then he asked Josh the question Josh had really, really hoped Rory would never ask.

"Josh, do you know where Annabelle is?"

Well, shit. Now he just had to decide whether he should lie to Rory and risk losing a potential friend, or whether to narc on Annabelle—and Justin. Evan too. There really wasn't any kind of decision to be made, and although Josh felt bad about it, he said, "Nope, sure don't," and figured it wasn't exactly a lie. He couldn't exactly pinpoint where she and Justin and Evan would be having sex right now, at least he couldn't do so with any sort of accuracy other than handing out his brother's address, and no way was Josh doing that.

"Josh..." Rory rumbled. "Come on, I know you know, and Annabelle's not answering her phone. I need to talk to her as soon as possible. So if you won't tell me where she is, and I am not gonna hate you for that, she is your best buddy after all, but can you at least have her call me? Please?"

"I'll try," Josh promised, dreading what he'd have to do to fulfil that promise. He said his goodbyes then called Justin. Annabelle was so gonna owe him for this.

Chapter Nineteen

"Ohhh, yeah...suck me, just like that...God!" Annabelle moaned and arched her back, thrusting her groin against Justin's mouth. Justin grinned around her clit and scraped his teeth over the hard little nubbin, feeling his own cock leak when cream from her pussy coated his fingers as he worked her inner walls. He flicked his gaze up and watched as Evan slowly fed his cock into Annabelle's mouth.

The sight of Evan's plump ass, the slight coat of fuzz over the taut flesh and the dusky line of his crease only fired Justin's need. He needed to bury his dick somewhere, and the options he had now were mind boggling. Evan's pucker winked at him as the man began thrusting deep into Annabelle's throat. The scent of Annabelle's arousal filled Justin's nostrils, tempting him to shove his length deep in the warm velvety tunnel, or he could...

Justin trailed his fingers from Annabelle's pussy to the soft skin below then further down until he reached the tight little rosette. Yeah, that's what he wanted, to feel her ass clenching around his dick as Evan filled her cunt with his thick rod. There was nothing quite like feeling Evan's length rubbing against his through the thin wall that separated the two openings. It was nasty and erotic, and more intense than any other way of making love. Justin teased around the knotty muscle, his nails catching gently at each fold. Annabelle bucked and let loose a strangled sound that was, despite being garbled by the mouthful of cock she had, a clear demand for more.

"I got you, baby," Justin promised. He pressed against the furled opening, sucking hard on Annabelle's clit to counter any discomfort she might feel. Annabelle's thighs quivered as Justin pushed his finger in to the first knuckle. "So fucking tight, hot," he lifted off her clit long enough to say, then promptly took the bead between his teeth as he sank his finger fully into her ass.

"Guhhh…"

Might have been a 'Gahhhd', Justin mused, or maybe Annabelle meant 'Good'. Either way, her inner muscles clamped around his digit, rippling as she ground her butt down, a silent plea for more. Justin flicked his tongue over her nub, a rapid staccato of sensual assault, pushing Annabelle closer to the edge. He heard Evan grunt, felt the bed bounce as Evan began to seriously fuck Annabelle's mouth. Justin glanced up to see Annabelle's hands clasping Evan's ass cheeks, her nails digging into the skin as she pulled him forward and encouraged him to give her more and give it harder.

Sliding a second finger into Annabelle's tight heat, Justin dropped his attention back to what he was doing. He worked Annabelle's clit as he finger-fucked her ass, corkscrewing his digits to loosen the silky vice his dick was throbbing to fill. Once he stretched her with three fingers, got her pink bud gaping for him, he could take her, bury his aching shaft inside and—

The headboard banging against the wall threw him off his rhythm. Apparently it did the same for Evan and Annabelle since they froze, both their bodies tensing up as if to flee. What the hell? More pounding while none of them were moving had the light bulb clicking on in Justin's head. Someone was at the bedroom door.

"Can you guys stop fucking long enough to answer your phones? Or doorbell? Or bedroom door?" Josh hollered through said door.

"Shit!"

"Fuck!"

"Well, not now," Justin sniped at Evan. He did, however, agree with Annabelle's heartily rasped 'shit'. Shit was what he was going to beat Josh into a pile of for interrupting just when he'd been fixing to—

"Rory needs to talk to Annabelle, now!" Josh pounded on the door. Justin shot up off the bed and ran for the door when he realised he hadn't locked it. There hadn't been any need, they were in their—well, in his and Evan's—own home, for shit's sake. Though if he had anything to say about it, it'd be Annabelle's, too, and soon.

The sight of the knob twisting was like something out of a nightmare. Icy fear teased Justin's spine. Josh *knew* what the three of them were doing, and Josh was a grown man, but fuck it all, Justin didn't want his little brother to see them like this!

"Get in the bathroom," Justin yelled at Evan and Annabelle. He grabbed the knob and used his greater weight to keep Josh on the other side of the door. The sound of four feet slapping against the floor sucked some of the tension from Justin's body, but it wasn't until he heard the soft *snick* of the bathroom door closing that Justin started to calm down. "Give me just a sec, Josh. I dunno what's so freaking important you have to barge in—"

Which was exactly what Josh did the second Justin stepped away from the door. Justin snarled and reached to cover his parts. Josh merely cocked a brow at him. "You have some...stuff, right about here." Josh pointed at his own chin. "I don't even want to know what it is, either. I'm going to replay this in my head over and over until I convince myself I walked in here and you were brushing your teeth, except that's not exactly white enough...oh gross!"

Justin would have snickered as Josh turned a couple of shades paler than his norm, but he was too mortified. Carefully keeping one hand over his cock, or over as much of it as he could, Justin swiped at Annabelle's juices. Then he snickered, and finally laughed until his eyes watered.

"Are you having some type of mental breakdown?" Josh asked in a very professional tone. "Or maybe it's loss of blood to the brain. Go...cover yourself with something so I don't have to see your icky nakedness, will you?"

Justin shook his head as Josh stared up at the ceiling. "It reeks of sex in here, which normally would be interesting, but since it's you, Evan and my best friend, it's just a very disturbing odour. I might be the one who has a breakdown if you don't hurry up."

That nearly set Justin off again, but he managed to pull on a pair of sweats and dig out pairs for Annabelle and Evan along with a couple of T-shirts as well. Josh could just deal with his chest. "I'm decent now," Justin said as he opened the bathroom door and tossed the clothes to Annabelle. Evan was washing her supple body with a wet rag, and Justin's cock flared back to full mast in a heartbeat.

"Jesus, can't you control that thing?" Josh snorted and started towards the bed then stopped. "I don't wanna sit there. That's like the bed of iniquity. I might catch bi cooties." Josh pivoted on his heel then walked over to the dresser, cocking one hip against the edge of the heavy oak top. Justin glanced down at his straining erection and decided wearing the biggest T-shirt he had wasn't a bad idea after all. He pulled one on as Evan and Annabelle came out of the bathroom. Both of them looked flushed with embarrassment, Justin thought. Then again, he didn't know what they might have been doing in there while he was hiding his willy from Josh.

Willy. Shit. Maybe he had suffered some brain damage if he was thinking of his dick in such juvenile terms. Justin reached out and took one of his lovers' hands in each of his own then led them to the bed. The sense of rightness as he held on to Annabelle and Evan, and was held in return, gentled some deeply buried part of himself Justin hadn't been aware existed. He knew at that moment he'd do anything to make their relationship work.

* * * *

Annabelle didn't embarrass easily, but she really thought she might melt into a puddle of mortified goop any second now. Before she could ask Josh what had sent him over here, Josh's cell rang. He plucked the phone out of his shirt pocket and answered it, looking startled as he listened.

"Those are some, er, bright scrubs," Evan muttered, earning a glare and a finger from Josh.

"Yeah I'm here with her now," Josh was saying, "no, I can't do that, but I can have—oh, okay. Sure." Josh listened for a few more seconds then squeaked, "Me? Why do you want me to—okay. Of course. We'll be there in an hour. Because that's the soonest we can get there!" He gnawed on his lower lip then as he looked at Annabelle. "Rory said he wouldn't hate me if I didn't tell him where Annabelle was, he just said he needed to talk to her, so quit asking me that. We'll be there as soon as we can, I promise." Josh disconnected the call and tucked his phone away. "That was Chance."

"Chance?" Annabelle stood up and started towards Josh, aware of Justin and Evan at her sides. "Is Rory okay? Is he hurt or—"

"No," Josh said, though Annabelle didn't think he sounded certain. "I spoke to him twice already, once when I was at lunch then again when I took off early to head over here. If *people* would *answer* their phones sometimes..."

"Not now, Josh," Justin ordered. Annabelle wanted to tell Justin not to bark at Joshie, but then again, she wasn't in the mood to be lectured either. "What did Rory want?"

Josh shrugged. "I don't know, he didn't sound particularly upset, more like concerned the first time he called me. The second time, though, he sounded, I dunno, rattled. This time, I thought..." Josh looked at the floor and crossed his arms over his chest. "I thought maybe I heard him in the background, crying, maybe. It could have been the TV, or someone else, or I could be wrong, but *Chance* called me, not Rory, and Chance was snarly and definitely pissed when I wouldn't tell him where we were and Rory had told me he didn't expect me to betray your confidences basically and even so there's Justin and Evan to consider and I—"

And he was in full babble mode. Annabelle pulled away from her lovers and snuggled up to her best friend, looping her arms around his neck. "Joshie, it's okay. Rory *wouldn't* expect you to narc on me, really, he wouldn't. Chance is probably just freaked out because something upset Rory." Which, frankly, scared the hell out of her. Rory wasn't a whimpering cry-baby, so if it *was* Rory Josh had heard in the background, what in the world could have upset him so? Did that fuckhead who'd hurt him—and Chance, and numerous other men and women—get out of prison somehow?

"We need to go." Annabelle stepped back and released Josh, who nodded sluggishly.

"We'll go with you if you need us to Annabelle, or want us to, even, but I don't know if now's the best time to break this to Rory," Evan said. "We'd really like to be there for you if you need us. Your brother, too, like...like family."

Evan blushed fiercely with the statement, and to Annabelle's amazement, so did Justin, but both men stared at her intently, telling her silently how much they meant it. "That's more than I ever expected anyone to do for me, and I"—*might be falling head over heels for you two*—"appreciate it more than I can say, but I think you're right Evan, now's not the time, especially since I don't have a clue what's going on."

Annabelle said quick goodbyes to Justin and Evan, promising to call them as soon as she could. She rushed from their house, ignoring the aches and pains that had seemed pleasant such a short while earlier.

Her mind was tossing up worst-case scenarios which she rejected almost instantly since they almost always involved Rory being hurt, or Chance. She was certain that wasn't the case, but Max or Bo...

Josh was silent on the drive for the most part, though he did occasionally murmur reassurances. And he ditched his usually cautious driving, keeping the gas pedal close to the floorboard. An hour's trip was cut down to forty five minutes, and Annabelle was a tangled wreck of nerves by the time they pulled up in front of the big house. She bolted from the car, Josh keeping up with her as they ran to the porch. It wasn't until Chance stepped outside that Annabelle realised she was still wearing Justin's—or Evan's, or maybe both men's—clothes, and she could still smell cum, or maybe that was her own paranoia.

Chance eyed her as critically as she did him when she stopped at the foot of the steps. For the first time since she'd met him, her brother's partner looked every bit his age. Deep grooves cut into the sides of his face by his mouth. The normally fine lines around Chance's eyes were more pronounced, the smooth brow was wrinkled, and he just looked exhausted, or like he was hurting. Annabelle's heart ached even as fear made her toes and fingers go numb.

"What? What is it?" Annabelle asked as she clutched at Josh's hand. Josh scooted closer to her, offering comfort and support with an ease only he ever seemed to have. Chance opened his mouth to answer but Rory appeared in the doorway and beat him to it. His words shocked Annabelle as much as his haggard, tear-streaked face did.

"Dad's dead."

Chapter Twenty

"Dad's dead?" Annabelle parroted, trying to make sense of those two words. It should have been easy enough to do, yet her mind blanked as she stared at her brother. Rory's red rimmed eyes and tear streaked cheeks sent his revelation roaring through her head, each word as loud as a sonic boom. An odd buzzing resounded in her ears as her pulse escalated.

"I've got you, sweetie." Annabelle nodded numbly as Josh released her hand and looped his arm around her shoulders instead. "Come on, let's go inside and snuggle on the couch, okay?"

Annabelle let Josh guide her up the steps and into the house. They settled on the love seat rather than the couch since Chance and Rory were on the larger piece of furniture.

Rory scrubbed at his cheeks then sniffled. Annabelle's own eyes were so dry they burned, but not because she wasn't hurting. The grief and loss were growing exponentially inside her with each breath she took. All the good, warm feelings she'd been wallowing in abandoned her with the realisation that there'd never be a chance for reconciliation with her father.

Logically, she knew it never would have happened anyway, but the little girl in her who wanted her daddy's approval had always hoped that one day he'd see how wrong he'd been and there'd be forgiveness, if not affection.

"He tried to call me today," Annabelle blurted out as another wave of guilt swelled. "I missed the call but when I saw it this morning on my phone, I just...I just ignored it—"

Chance made a slicing gesture with his hand. "It wasn't Ian who called you. It was probably the same guy who called us in the middle of the night, some guy by the name of Carlos Navarra."

Annabelle frowned as she went over the people and ranch hands she knew. The name didn't ring a bell.

"I didn't recognise the name either," Rory said, his voice cracking as more tears leaked from his eyes. "He said...Ian...Dad died almost a month ago."

The desert-dry feeling vanished as Annabelle's eyes flooded. Her vision blurred and she opened her mouth to ask how, why, something, but a sob burst free instead. This was worse, so much worse than just their father dying. Annabelle curled into herself, hunching as blade-sharp agony ripped through her.

She cried until her head felt thick and heavy, her nose stuffy and her throat raw. Her hands ached from her clenching them into tight fists, and she slowly became aware of being held. Rory cradled her in his lap, his own grief and pain matching hers shudder for shudder, sob for sob.

"What happened to Dad?" She croaked once she could get the words out. "Who is Carlos Navarra?" *Why didn't anyone notify us sooner?*

"Aneurysm," Chance answered when Rory didn't speak. "It was very quick. And Carlos Navarra..." Chance glanced away, his lips pinched tightly together.

Rory cleared his throat and tipped Annabelle's head up. She nearly lost it again looking into his midnight blue eyes. "Carlos Navarra is the new foreman, hired by the man Dad left the ranch to."

Annabelle's stomach dipped with a sense of prescience. Rory's words didn't shock her as they should have. The only thing she felt was completely numb.

"Dad left the ranch to a son he had before he ever married Mom," Rory rasped. "We have a half-brother, and he never said a word to us about it!"

It didn't surprise her. Their father had been a cruel, manipulative man. He'd have got a real kick out of keeping them away from their brother, then blindsiding them with the knowledge of said brother's existence after the old man died. Wherever the mean bastard was, he would be laughing his ass off.

"He probably meant to leave the ranch to this...this brother of ours all along," Annabelle said. Rory mumbled an agreement. Annabelle slid off his lap and looked at Chance. He was less affected by this and therefore the more clearheaded of the bunch, besides Josh, but Josh didn't know anything about her dad, not really.

"What else did Navarra have to say?"

Chance's eyes narrowed as his expression shifted into one of anger. "He said Ian left the ranch to his other son, and that none of the ranch hands had called because they were pretty much loyal to Ian. The new guy — your, uh, brother, fired them all first thing. As for Navarra, he wouldn't even tell me this brother's name, said part of him inheriting was that he couldn't have contact with us. Navarra said he would have called sooner but there was nothing with our numbers on it, nothing pertaining to you or Rory at all in the house."

Rory turned misery laden eyes towards her. "Dad wiped us from it as if we never existed."

Annabelle had so many questions to ask, but they wouldn't quit spinning around in her head long enough for her to grasp them. She settled for the first one she could think of. "Why this Navarra guy? Where was our...brother," *shit, that is messed up!* "Where was he while this was going on?"

"Now, there's a question I wondered myself, but Rory needed me, and this Navarra guy was in an all-fired hurry to get off the phone. I don't have an answer for that. Wish I did."

"Dad would make not talking to us a condition for our mystery brother to inherit the ranch," Rory muttered. "Anything to hurt us. Maybe even hurt the son he decided to claim."

Annabelle agreed with Rory's assessment. That's exactly something their father would have done. Even dead, he'd manipulate them if possible. "Rory, do you want to challenge the will?" Annabelle held her breath as Rory considered her question. She hoped...

Rory finally shook his head. "No. I don't want the place, I don't want Dad's money, none of it. I wanted his respect, his love, but we both know that would never have happened. I loved him because he was my father, but sometimes I hated him for it, too."

"Me, too," Annabelle admitted. "Does that make us horrible people?"

"No," Josh pitched in, "That makes you both human. You *might* have been horrible people if you high-fived each other and danced to celebrate his death."

Annabelle gave her best buddy a watery smile as she laid her head on his shoulder. Chance and Rory excused themselves and left the room to check in with Max and Bo.

"You'll be all right, sweetie," Josh muttered as he stroked her back. "You have a lot of people who love you, and you have Justin and Evan, who both care about you a great deal. You really should give them a call as soon as you're up to it and tell them what's happened. Justin has been texting me nonstop, and the last several texts have been rather bitchy 'cause I won't tell him what's going on. Not my place to," he tacked on when she started to ask why. "That's gotta be either a blessing or a curse of a ménage, having two people to fret over you."

A strangled sound from the living room doorway startled both Annabelle and Josh. Her head snapped up and clipped Josh's chin. Shards of pain spread from the point of impact as she looked up to find her brother staring at her with a horrified expression on his face.

Fuck! She'd hoped to have time to break her new relationship to Rory gently, but it was too late now. His eyes narrowed into thin slits as his cheeks turned ruddy. Annabelle braced herself for the coming explosion.

Rory's thunderous look darkened as he stepped into the room. "Annabelle, what the *fuck* is Josh talking about? He'd better be joking or someone..." Rory blanched then, though she'd have sworn it impossible, he looked even more furious. "Several *someones* are going to be getting their asses kicked."

"Oh shit," Josh whispered.

Yeah, oh shit indeed.

Chapter Twenty-One

The fury that rolled through her wasn't all for Rory—or maybe it was, because that hot ball of anger spewed up before Rory even finished speaking. Annabelle wasn't thinking about her dad, or the mysterious new brother who lucked out and got it all.

No, as she glared at Rory, she was thinking, *here's the one person I thought I could always count on, the one I walked away from the ranch for when that ranch could have been mine, the one I didn't judge or sneer at, and in return for all of that, for unconditional love and constant support, I get this shit in return?*

"Is it true?" Rory demanded. "Are you fucking two guys at the same time? The three of you—" he stopped and shook his head, curling his lips into a grimace. "I can't believe you'd do something like that. Are you just trying to out-do me, find something that would have pissed Dad off worse than me being gay? Because I think you might have succeeded!"

The attack from Rory may have seemed mild to someone who didn't know him, but for the normally calm, loving man she knew her brother to be—had thought him to be—each word was like a poison barb digging into her soul. Rory had never spoken to her like this, not even when she'd insisted on moving out of his and Chance's home and into the bunkhouse. They'd argued then, but it hadn't been a personal attack that left her bleeding inside. Annabelle hated the way Rory hurt her so easily, and she turned her pain into anger, the way she always had. It rolled through her and filled her in hot and cold flashes through her veins.

Annabelle was so furious she actually felt calm, a dangerous occurrence. She stood and shook off Josh's attempts to stop her from moving, and two long strides had her in front of her brother. Rory tensed as his mouth pinched into a tight line, his nostrils flared with each breath, and he was vibrating with indignation, or self-righteousness, or something else that, combined with his appearance, reminded Annabelle of a pissy bull. Any second now he'd start snorting and pawing at the floor. "What makes you think you have the right to judge me, or Justin, or Evan?" Annabelle asked, seething as she glared at Rory. "How dare you, when I've never once done that to you?"

"It's different! I never went out and fucked two guys at the same time!" Rory closed his eyes for a moment then didn't look at Annabelle when he opened them again. "Chance is the second man I've been with, and he'll be the last. I can't understand doing something— Annabelle, I can't understand why you're doing this! I'm trying not to make it about you being a woman, but you know there's still that double standard and if people find out you're screwing two guys, and if those guys are, you know, together, do you know how hateful people can be about stuff like that?"

"I'm seeing how you're being about it, aren't I?" Annabelle retorted as she moved closer to Rory. "And it shouldn't matter if I'm a woman, your sister, whoever! It's my life and what and who I chose to do behind closed doors is no one else's business!"

"It doesn't work that way!" Rory shouted, his face turning almost purple as he did so. "They don't care if it's in private, you should know that!"

She did know that, but living her life by someone else's standards wasn't going to happen. Not even if those standards were her brother's. "And I don't care if they don't care! I'm not changing for you or them. It's not like I'm out fucking everything that has a dick, either. There are two men, two men I actually feel something for—and yes, it's more than lust. I don't know how much more, and I'm not willing to walk away an never find out. I suggest you deal with it, or maybe you want to cut me off like our father did us?" The thought added to the fear she'd tried so hard to ignore, and Annabelle shivered slightly as she stopped in front of Rory.

"Annabelle, maybe now's not the best time—" Josh began at her side.

Annabelle waved a hand to silence him while staring her brother down. This close, she could see the worry and fear etched into his expression, and her temper cooled a few degrees. This was her brother, she reminded herself, her sweet, innocent, idealistic brother who thought everyone had a soul mate. Maybe that was so, but Annabelle couldn't help but believe some people had at least two.

"Maybe Josh is right and this is the wrong time, but there's no help for it now, not with you looking at me like I'm some kind of slut. I'm not." Annabelle took a deep breath, knowing she'd need it to push the rest of her words out. "What is happening between me, Evan, and Justin is something more than getting together to have sex. I care about them a great deal, and they feel the same for me."

Rory looked sceptical for a long moment, then his shoulders slumped as he glanced away. "I just don't see how this...something like this can be good for you. I don't want you hurt."

Well, God damn it, there went the rest of her mad, leaving her feeling sad and hurt. Annabelle let her arm drop and she took a step back. "You hurt me, Rory, with the way you reacted, the things you said. Justin and Evan haven't."

Annabelle turned around and slammed into Chance's broad chest. He gripped her arms and steadied but didn't let go once she'd found her footing. Annabelle looked at him and wished to hell she could tell what he was thinking.

"If I heard correctly, you're in a ménage."

She doubted 'Duh' would be a prudent response, so Annabelle merely nodded. Chance darted a glance at Rory before focusing his attention back on her.

"I think you can see how that might shock someone who cares about you, especially if that person is as innocent about things like that as Rory is."

"I guess," Annabelle muttered, feeling unjustly scolded. It wasn't like she'd decked Rory or anything, though the thought had crossed her mind.

"And added onto the news about y'all's dad, it's probably a lot to take in for someone like him." Chance looked at Rory again, and this time Annabelle could read the apology on Chance's face. "He's not like us, or the way I used to be, at least. Rory can't separate love from sex. They go together for him."

Yeah, she knew that. "He looked disgusted."

Chance grunted, his hands tightening briefly around her biceps. "Your brother loves you. Are you serious about these other guys, or are y'all just having some fun? There's nothing wrong with either of those things as long as everyone involved agrees to what's going on."

"Did you miss the part where I said I cared about Justin and Evan? And they care about me, too?" Maybe Chance had selective hearing.

Chance's lips twitched before stretching into a grin. "No, I didn't, but I thought it might be a good thing for Rory to hear it again." Chance's amusement faded as he looked at Josh. "Would this Justin happen to be the brother you've told us about?"

Josh looked like he was considering making a run for it. He was all big eyes and slack-jawed fear. In other words, he wasn't very coherent. Annabelle answered for him. "That would be the Justin, yeah, and his partner Evan." She craned her neck around to glance at Rory, who was looking less and less angry and more than a little confused. "And they don't play. They are very serious about finding the right woman for them. We're trying to figure out if that's me." She was both hopeful and terrified that it may be so.

Chance let her go. "I think Rory just needs a little time to digest everything. Why don't you go on back to your men, although"—Chance smirked as he looked her over from head to toe—"You might want to change into some of your clothes so you can give those nappy things you're wearing back to whichever boyfriend of yours lent them to you."

Annabelle's natural inclination to make others see what she wanted them to made it difficult, but she finally nodded. "I'll do that." She turned to her brother and wished she could give him a hug, but she wasn't sure how he'd react. "Let me know when you're ready to talk," she told Rory. "I don't want to lose you over this. I don't want to lose them. Don't make me choose."

There was nothing for it now but for her to leave, so she did, her heart aching over Rory's reaction. Surely he'd come around.

Annabelle was opening the bunkhouse door when the front screen door squeaked then popped back into place as the sound of heavy footfalls caused her to pause. She turned and found Rory standing only inches away.

"I don't understand," Rory said, "but I'd like to. I love you, Sis." He pulled her in for the hug she wanted so badly. "I'm sorry I was a jerk. I'll do better. As long as these guys make you happy, that's good enough for me."

Annabelle smiled as tears slid down her cheeks. Josh had kind of done her a favour, forcing her to come clean to Rory. She owed him big time for that. Now she just had to think of a way to repay him.

Chapter Twenty-Two

Annabelle walked into her bedroom. She looked at the bare walls and unadorned surfaces. There was nothing on her dresser, and the only things on the nightstand were an alarm clock and the lamp. The bedding was a blah shade of beige. She hadn't bothered with curtains for the window, only a cheap plastic blind from Walmart. All in all, the room was depressing and didn't reflect anything of herself.

Had she always seen this place as a temporary resting point? Or was she just too worn out at the end of the workday to bother with decorating? Maybe she should ask Josh...Annabelle snorted. Like that wasn't stereotyping. Josh was gay and therefore must be eager to decorate and damn good at it. She knew better, she'd seen his apartment. Josh's fondness for hot pink didn't stop with his favourite scrubs. Neither did his love of penguins.

"Are you okay?"

Annabelle turned to find Josh giving her an odd look. Was she okay? Truthfully, she was a little unwilling to delve too deep into her mind and emotions to check. "I'm fine. Just thinking this room has the personality of a snail. Or not even."

Josh gave the room a long, critical look. "It needs something. Colour, maybe—"

Annabelle cringed.

"Pink."

"I think I'll pass." Annabelle walked to her dresser and started to dig out fresh underwear. She'd already cleared taking the day off with Chance yesterday, but she realised as she thought about it, that she just didn't feel right running off to spend time with Evan and Justin when her brother was so obviously torn up over their dad's death. She wasn't sure how she felt about it. A dull ache kept trying to start in her chest, and her mind kept trying to grab for whatever good memories she had of her father.

There weren't many. The time Annabelle had helped birth a calf that had got stuck, and when she'd left college to return to the ranch. Her dad had actually slapped her on the back then and told her he was glad she was back where she'd belonged. Annabelle had been angry then, feeling like she'd been reprimanded for leaving, but now she wondered if the old man might have actually missed her. Had he ever loved her or Rory?

"I can't think about this right now." And if she went back to Justin and Evan's house, she'd have to. They'd have questions she wasn't ready to answer yet.

"Hey sweetie," Josh said as he put his arm around her shoulders. "I know it's been a rough day for you. If there's anything I can do to help, just say so."

Annabelle turned and embraced Josh, resting her head on his shoulder. "Goes both ways, Joshie. You never told me about whoever marked you."

Josh snickered as he hugged her tight enough to force the air from her lungs. "Ah, diversion. Well I will let you get away with it this time and tell you the jackass who hoovered my neck is history. He doesn't matter, we never had sex, he was a great gaping mistake."

Josh tried to keep his tone light, but Annabelle heard the pain and anger buried in his voice. "I'm sorry, Joshie. You point him out if he shows up at the Xxchange and I will castrate the fucker for you. I'll use toenail clippers so it'll take a while."

"It's a deal." Josh rubbed her back then met her gaze when Annabelle raised her head. "So, you're staying here with Rory, aren't you?"

"Yeah, I think I need to." Annabelle released Josh and turned back to dig out the clean clothes she needed. "He's my brother, and he's hurting. Justin and Evan are..." *the sexiest fuckers I've ever known, under my skin, in my head and –* "I don't know what they are, what the three of us are, but finding out will have to wait. I can't leave Rory right now." Annabelle piled the clothes into her arms then turned to Josh. She bumped the dresser drawer shut with her hip. "And if Rory's up to it, he and I need to have a chat about this long lost brother or whatever the hell he is. Maybe we can call the ranch, talk to Navarra."

"You're not running from Justin and Evan again are you?" Josh asked a question Annabelle was, even at that moment, asking herself. She scrubbed at her forehead as she seriously considered her motivations.

"No, I think Rory and I need to spend some time together. I hope Evan and Justin understand, but if they don't..." Annabelle shrugged. Anyone who expected her to choose between them and Rory wasn't worth her time. She didn't think Justin or Evan was like that, but since they kept fucking more than talking, she couldn't be sure.

Josh rolled his eyes and batted his lashes at her. "They'll be fine with it. Neither would expect you to ditch your brother at a time like this."

"Goof," Annabelle muttered. "I need to get cleaned up then hunt my brother down."

"And I need to go back to work and make up for the time I took off early. Give me a hug."

Annabelle stepped into Josh's arms and did him one better, giving him a slobbery kiss on the cheek.

"Ewww, gross!" Josh leapt back and gave her a mock glare as he swiped at the spot. "Why did you do that? Keep your body fluids to yourself!" For all his mock indignation, Josh was grinning from ear to ear.

Annabelle laughed and shoo'd him towards the door. "Go on now, before I put you to mucking stalls!"

Once Josh was gone, Annabelle hopped in the shower and washed away the traces of her night with Justin and Evan. She was towelled off and dressed in a matter of minutes, then she went to find her brother, dialling Justin's number as she walked towards the house. Justin's voicemail came on so Annabelle stuttered out a message about her brother needing her then ended the call.

Annabelle bounded up the porch steps and tapped at the front door. Chance was almost immediately on the other side of it, pulling open the screen to gesture her inside.

"How's he doing?"

Chance shook his head. "I don't know. One minute he seems fine, then he's back to crying. I don't know how to help him deal with this."

"Just be with him," Annabelle advised. "He's older than me by eighteen months, but in some ways he still seems so much younger."

Chance nodded as he hooked his arm through hers. "All right, I can do that, and so can you."

* * * *

It was almost midnight by the time Annabelle left Chance and Rory's. Justin had called hours ago and she'd given him the bare bones version of today's events when she'd stepped outside for a little privacy. Rory hadn't asked her any more questions about the two men she was involved with, instead spending hours talking about their dad and wondering why he'd been such a cruel man. But when she'd taken Justin's call, she could feel Rory's gaze on her through the window, and she wondered if he really was going to try to accept the fledgeling relationship she was entering. She hoped so; when she thought about the choice she might have to make if he didn't, something close to panic swelled in her. She couldn't give her brother up, and even though she wasn't sure how serious Justin and Evan were, she knew she was feeling a lot more for both men than she'd ever thought she'd feel for anyone.

Twice the men, twice the intensity. Annabelle stripped and dropped into bed, pulling the sheet over her body. It was too hot for the blanket.

Annabelle squirmed and shoved at her pillows, but she couldn't get comfortable and she was afraid she knew why. One night spent cuddling between two gorgeous men seemed to have spoilt her. Stupid to be so invested so quickly, but it was what it was and there was nothing she could do to stop it. She wanted Evan and Justin, wanted to be with them right now —

"Fuck!" Annabelle sat up in the bed and looked at the alarm clock. It was after midnight, too late to call Justin like she'd said she would. Still, he'd be pissed if she didn't do something, so she grabbed her cell off the nightstand and sent a text to him and Evan both, explaining that she thought it too late to call them. Her phone rang before she could set it back down. Annabelle yelped and slapped her free hand over her heart as she glared at the phone's display.

Justin, you dick! Nearly gave me a heart attack! Not that she was mad. Pure joy rushed from her head to her toes, warming her already hot skin and sending all sorts of body parts throbbing. Annabelle tapped the answer button and set the phone to her ear.

"Are you trying to kill me?" Annabelle asked, ruining it by snickering through the accusation.

"You about worried me and Justin to death, so we're even," Evan hollered, sounding kind of tinny over the phone. "You're on speaker, by the way."

Well, that explains the hollow sound to Evan's voice. "I didn't mean to." And she wasn't going to apologise for spending time with her brother. "Rory and I had a lot to talk about."

"We understand, Evan wasn't criticising," Justin soothed, and Annabelle couldn't hold back a gasp as liquid heat pooled in her cunt. Justin must have been closer to the phone. His deep baritone sent a vibration of lust rippling over her skin. "You do what you need to. We just...we missed you, is all."

Annabelle was stunned for a moment, then her heart started pounding, pushing the happy feeling growing in her through her bloodstream. "I missed y'all too."

That wasn't as hard to admit as she'd feared it would be.

"How much?" Justin's voice dipped impossibly lower, warming with desire at the same time.

"Enough that I couldn't sleep," Annabelle said, shocking herself even. "That's probably more than you're ready to hear, both of you, but—"

"No, no it isn't," Evan exclaimed, now sounding as close to the phone as Justin. "That's exactly what we needed to hear. God, I wish you were here." Justin echoed Evan's wish and Annabelle felt a lightness inside she hadn't ever experienced, as if helium filled her completely.

"Rory knows about us," Annabelle confessed, though why right then she couldn't say. "He didn't handle it so well at first, but then he apologised and said he'd do better."

"Do you believe him? Was he saying that just to keep you from coming back here?" Justin asked after a long silence that undid all the warm fuzzy feelings Annabelle had been enjoying.

"He's not a liar," Annabelle snapped, then continued, speaking over Justin and Evan. "Rory's sweet and kind of naïve about…about sex, in a way, though I think Chance is educating him on the subject at least a couple of times a day. Still, they're in a monogamous relationship, so Rory doesn't really have any comprehension of a ménage. And I sure as shit don't have a lot, but even I would know better than to insult your brother."

Justin sighed loud enough to make Annabelle want to snap at him again. If he was going to give her crap over her outburst…

"I'm sorry," Justin said, and Annabelle thought her eyes might pop out of her head. She snapped her mouth shut as Justin spoke again. "I shouldn't have said anything like that. It's not an excuse, but I was — am still, to tell the truth — afraid of what you'd do if Rory didn't accept us. We don't want to lose you."

Shit, my emotions are swinging up and down and up again so fast I can't keep track of them! Annabelle was thrumming with joy, and she bet she probably even glowed a little. "It's not going to come to that. Chance understands, he'll talk to my brother. I think he's had a ménage or two in the past, although probably not for long. He didn't do long term until Rory."

Annabelle heard murmuring between Justin and Evan but she couldn't make out their conversation. Justin filled her in quickly though.

"Evan wants to know if you're naked..." Justin exhaled, his breath a shaky rasp that fuelled Annabelle's rekindled arousal. "And so do I. We're both laying here in bed butt nekkid, horny as hell, thinking about you."

Annabelle lay back on her pillow and plucked at one nipple, drawing out a shuddering breath of her own as she thought of her two studs naked in bed. "I'm not wearing a damn thing other than the sheet. If you two are so horny, why haven't y'all — "

"Because it's the three of us," Evan stated firmly. "We weren't going to get off together. But now..."

Justin moaned and Annabelle felt more cream slick her pussy. "Tell me." She put the phone on speaker and lay it by her head then pinched both of her nipples between her thumbs and forefingers.

Justin answered in a strained voice, speaking between pants. "Ev is...oh God...he's got my dick crammed into his throat and...yes, baby, do it!" Justin cried out and Annabelle whimpered as she desperately tried to picture the two men and what they were doing. She pinched her nipples harder, needing the firmer touch her lovers could so expertly administer. Annabelle spread her legs wide open then cupped her breasts, squeezing the handfuls as her hips jerked.

"Tell me," she demanded, except it came out more as an aching plea. "Tell me, please."

Justin was moaning and gasping almost constantly. Annabelle heard a lewd slurp that had her reaching for her clit.

"I have two fingers in Justin's ass," Evan rasped, "and I'm fucking him hard as I can, making him feel it like he likes to."

"Oh fuck, I want to see that." Annabelle flicked her clit then slid her fingers lower to pull at her slick lips. She hadn't thought Justin liked to receive ass play, he seemed so toppy, but his moans were even louder now, and Annabelle wanted to play along.

"Show you next time," Evan grunted, "or as soon as his sweet ass can handle it. You fingering your cunt yet?"

Annabelle shivered and pushed the tips of two fingers into her wet sex. "Yes, fuck, Evan, Justin…" She thrust her fingers in deeper, but the achy needy feeling in her didn't seem to notice. "Not enough, Evan…"

"Fuck! You have a toy, a fat dildo or vibrator?" Evan was breathing heavy now, his voice so rough Annabelle wouldn't have recognised it. "I have three fingers in him now, fixing to make it four—"

Justin's groan was loud and beautiful, the agony of arousal at a perfect pitch. Annabelle ached to be there with them. She stretched her arm and fumbled for the nightstand drawer. Opening it was tricky at the angle she was laying, but she found the big blue vibrator that she used occasionally.

"Got it." Annabelle didn't bother with the lube. Her cunt was wet enough, and if there was that burn of friction, so much the better. "Going to fuck myself with it and imagine it's both of you, though it isn't big enough."

"Shit!" Justin shouted and Evan laughed, a pleased, loving sound that spurred Annabelle on.

"You just made our lover shoot his load before he wanted to," Evan crooned. "Now he's going to suck me until I flood his mouth with my cum."

"Do it. Want to hear you lose it." She wedged the thick vibrator between her thighs and pushed the first few inches in. "Uhn. Not enough…"

"Push it in, fill that needy pussy up," Justin's rough voice ordered.

"That's enough talking," Evan said, "I've got better uses for your mouth right now, Jus. Do it, Belle, right now, when I'm shoving my dick in Justin's mouth."

Annabelle murmured what she hoped was an agreement as she pushed her toy through her slick folds until only the base remained outside her body. Nine inches of silicone cock filled her, and it should have dulled the emptiness in her cunt but she wanted…needed her men and told them as much.

"Soon, honey, if you want us there, we'll be there in under an hour—Jesus Christ! Jus!"

"Can't…not yet," Annabelle mumbled as she began fucking herself, thrusting the vibrator in hard and fast. It wasn't the same as having Justin and Evan in her, but the aggressive way she was working the toy was taking the edge off, and Evan's curses and grunts helped as well. Annabelle brought her other hand to her clit and began pressing down on the bead, sending white hot streaks of pleasure from her pussy to her knees and up to her tits. Which needed to be sucked and bit, but her hands were otherwise occupied.

"Fuck, Belle, you should see the way Justin's mouth is stretched wide around my dick, the way he —" Evan broke off with a gasp that turned into a shout. "Fucking hell! Belle, honey, soon —"

Annabelle twisted the vibrator inside her pussy and flicked the base, setting the vibrations to high as she rubbed her clit. Lightning struck the base of her spine then shot up its length as she cried out, unable to warn her lovers as her climax slammed into her with a suddenness and fierceness that stole her breath.

Evan's answering yell was peppered with curses, words like 'Fuck' and 'Damn' blended with 'Take it all' and 'Yeah, Jus, God!'

Annabelle gasped, drawing air in her deprived lungs as she shuddered and rubbed her climax out, her other hand pumping the vibrator in short, deep strokes. A last, violent burst of ecstasy seared under her skin and she screamed again as her vision dimmed to a dull grey.

Slowly she became aware of two things. She was still on the phone with her lovers, and she'd just put on a hell of a show for Max and Bo to listen to. Annabelle felt her cheeks burn then she burst out laughing, unable to stop herself when she thought of Max and Bo listening to that hot little phone sex session. No doubt they'd heard Justin and Evan too, though whether they heard clearly enough to know she was involved with two men, Annabelle didn't have a clue.

"What's so funny?" Evan asked, sounding as if he'd swallowed a load of gravel.

Annabelle snickered as she pulled out her toy and set it beside her hip. "Forgot I have bunkhouse mates."

She fell asleep to the amused laughter of her lovers.

Chapter Twenty-Three

Annabelle cracked an eyelid open as she slapped at the alarm clock. Despite having pretty much passed out after the phone sex — which had been hotter than a lot of the actual physical sex she'd had before meeting Justin and Evan — Annabelle had only slept soundly for about an hour. The rest of the night had been spent tossing and turning, her body unable to rest when her mind just wouldn't shut off. The result was she now felt like she'd been beaten with a baseball bat. Her muscles were stiff and achy, and her head...the entire goddamned thing throbbed and felt too heavy to lift. Surely her neck would snap under the weight of it.

On top of the physical complaints, Annabelle now found herself inundated with a barrage of emotional issues. She'd always thought herself able to keep a tight rein on the emotions that other people frequently gave over to — with the exception of anger, she knew *that* particular emotion got the better of her more often than it should have—but now she felt as if she might burst into tears at any moment. It was as if yesterday, she'd been able to focus on Rory and his needs, and somehow she'd thought...well. Annabelle snorted, which made her moan when the throbbing behind her eyes ramped up and threatened to shoot them out of their sockets. Obviously she wasn't so invincible after all.

"God damn it all," Annabelle muttered, her tongue tripping over the curse. Her mouth felt desert-dry, and her throat didn't feel any better. She rolled to her side and gingerly kicked off the sheet. The muted sounds of Max and Bo's voices reached her and Annabelle's eyes flew open as memories of how loud she and her lovers had been last night. Heat crawled over her skin, setting her cheeks to burning. "Oh fuck." Annabelle flopped over onto her back and rubbed at her temples. There was no way Max was going to be able to look at her, and Bo would probably snicker and tease her all day, although maybe not as bad as he would if she hadn't just yesterday received news of her dad's death.

A tap on her door had Annabelle sitting up and scrambling to grab the sheet. She flopped back on the mattress when she remembered she'd locked the door when she'd come to bed.

Bo's amused voice slipped through the door as he tapped at the door again. "Come on, Annabelle, I want all the details about—oh come on, Max, you gotta be curious too!"

Annabelle listened to the scuffle of footsteps outside her door. Snickers and soft thuds made her think the two men were horsing around. Clearly, her sexcapades hadn't kept *them* from getting enough sleep. The scuffling noises stopped after a louder thump on the door nearly rattled the thing off its hinges. Annabelle shoved aside her discomfort and got up, wrapping the sheet around her as best she could. Then a low moan filtered through the silence, followed quickly by another, rougher moan. Annabelle stopped and narrowed her eyes at the crack under the bedroom door. Looked like there was a four-footed beast out there.

Alrighty then. They definitely aren't fighting. Annabelle bit back the impulse to holler at Max and Bo and tell them to quit going at it against her door. Best just to get ready for work. Hopefully the shower would drown out the guys' noises.

* * * *

Bo was the only one in the kitchen when Annabelle walked in. The knowing glint in his eyes had her cheeks warming in an instant. He winked and grabbed her coffee mug, filling it with the rich brew he made so well.

"Max was too chicken to hang around," Bo said as he turned and handed her the cup of coffee. "I'm to pry all the details out of you — not the ones about what y'all did, we could hear all that clear enough" — Annabelle thought she might melt into an embarrassed puddle of goo right there in the kitchen as Bo continued — "and while het sex isn't our thing, I gotta admit, hearing you and" — Bo arched one brow up higher than anyone ought to be able to as he smirked — "two guys, wasn't it? Well, that was kind of hotter than hell. Sit down and dish, sweetie."

Annabelle concentrated on not sloshing any of her coffee out as she pulled out a chair and took a seat. She took a gulp of the hot brew, her eyes watering as it scorched her tongue and the roof of her mouth, then burnt all the way down to her stomach.

Bo snickered as he sat beside her. "Need it bad enough to risk a burn?"

"Yeah," Annabelle muttered before she took a much smaller sip. "I'm bracing myself for the inquisition."

"Oh now," Bo managed after he stopped laughing. "I'm not that bad, and you don't have to tell me anything, but"—he shrugged as the amusement fled his features—"I might be able to help. I have a couple of friends who've been in long term ménages. Never been in one myself, not for more than a night, but..."

Annabelle set her cup down and studied her fingers as hope chased off some of the fear that had been pressing at her. "So they can work? I mean, other than the sex part, 'cause that is all fine." Better than fine, but Bo probably knew that.

Bo smirked but his eyes held a kindness that made Annabelle's eyes water as intensely as the scalding coffee had. "Sounded like that part went past fine, and yeah, I've got a handful of friends in ménages, and three of those relationships have lasted over twenty years. Longer than most monogamous relationships. If you want, I can check my friends and see if they'd be willing to answer any questions you might have. I imagine they would, they're all pretty good guys."

Annabelle shifted in her seat as she considered the offer. "Maybe. I don't know. Are they all guys, the ménages?"

Bo shook his head. "Nope. One of them is like yours, and they've been together a long time. Probably, if you were willing, you could talk to them in person, see how it works for them. Pete, Macy, and Camden live on the outskirts of San Antonio, not too far. I can give them a call tonight after work."

"I'll think about it and let you know." Knowing there were other threesomes that flourished helped a lot in itself.

"So does Rory know?"

Annabelle nodded as she took another sip of coffee. She cradled the cup in her hands and looked at Bo. "Yeah, and he freaked at first. He found out by accident when he walked in on me and Joshie talking about it. It got ugly pretty quick, then Chance appeared and played referee. Hopefully Rory meant it when he said he'd try to accept it."

"Well," Bo said as he sat back in his chair. "That was probably a huge shock for your brother. On top of everything else, he finds out his little sister is not only not a virgin, but she's got two men, too. I think Rory's a bit innocent in some ways. Chance, on the other hand, not so much."

"Exactly. I was afraid Rory wouldn't be able to handle me being involved with Justin and Evan, and I didn't want to have to choose between them." Didn't know if she could, despite the loyalty she felt for her brother.

"Justin's the guy who was here a couple weeks ago?" Bo asked, and Annabelle didn't miss the appreciative gleam in his eyes. "He the same Justin who happens to be Josh's brother?"

"Yeah, to both" Annabelle waited for the next question, because she could see it forming on Bo's lips. "Is this Evan guy as good looking as Justin?" Bo was grinning again as he reached out and tugged at her hair. "Ooh, damn. I guess they aren't twins, that would have been even hotter—"

"Oh gross," Annabelle snickered. "No, that would have been *icky*. I don't get those fantasies." Although now, thanks to Bo, the idea of two Justins or two

Evans was pretty damned interesting. Still, she'd rather have one of each.

"So you think it's serious, the three of you?" Bo asked.

"Yeah," Annabelle answered, "they want it to be. Neither Justin or Evan is the kind who wants to play once then walk away. They're both looking for something special and seem to think they've found it in me."

"And what do *you* think?"

Annabelle thought she was the one who'd found something special. Now she just had to be brave enough to reach out and take it.

Chapter Twenty-Four

Four days, Annabelle thought, it'd only been four days since she'd left Evan and Justin's place. Four days since she'd touched her men or been touched by them. Four days that she, Rory, and Chance had been trying to find out more about Ian's death and the son he'd left the ranch to. Four days of Josh coming over and doing all sorts of things on the Internet she was kind of afraid might be illegal, and each effort on Josh's part proved fruitless. Four days of learning absofuckinglutely nothing. There hadn't even been a freaking obit for them to read online.

Their dad's lawyer wouldn't take their calls, and every phone number she or Rory had for the ranch lines had been changed. Their attempts to reach any of the former hands were just as unsuccessful, which didn't surprise either of them since their dad had supplied work cell phones for his hands. He'd liked to control every aspect of his employees' lives he possibly could. Now that those hands were no longer working at the Mossy Glenn, Annabelle didn't have a clue how to get hold of them. It was frustrating as hell, and on top of it all, Annabelle had an almost constant dull ache in her chest that she *knew* wouldn't let up until she was with Justin and Evan again. Talking to them on the phone helped some, but it wasn't enough. She was getting meaner than a badger and wasn't surprised at all when Chance called her on the radio and told her to get her ass into his office, *now*.

Annabelle was careful to bury her irritation — okay, bitchiness, she knew what she was feeling — deep as she brushed out Juju. Another new addition to the ranch, Juju was a gorgeous tovero paint, and eventually, Annabelle hoped to talk Chance into breeding the mare with Manilo and selling her the colt. Annabelle let the smooth coat and soft nickers calm her; there was just something about Juju when she was being brushed out that soothed Annabelle at least as much as it did the mare.

Reluctantly, Annabelle untied Juju and led her to her stall. She made sure Juju had plenty of food and water, and dug a carrot from the bucket stocked daily. Juju whinnied and tossed her head, prancing in place as she waited for her treat.

"You're a special girl, aren't you, Juju?" Annabelle handed over the carrot and rubbed the velvety soft patch above Juju's nose. "I'd buy you from Chance if I had the money. Maybe someday."

By the time Annabelle knocked on the door frame of the office, she was full of plans for her favourite mare. Chance's short "Come in," pulled her right out of those pleasant daydreams.

"You wanted to speak to me?" Annabelle figured that was more polite than 'You ordered me here, you grumpy prick?' Besides, she was the one whose fuse had been getting shorter and shorter. Chance gave her a narrow-eyed look and pointed at the seat across from his desk. Annabelle plopped down and kept her gaze locked with her boss's.

Chance finally quit giving her that hard look and sighed. "I know you've had a rough week…"

Annabelle snorted before she could think better of it. A rough week? He had no idea.

"Look," Chance began as he leant back in his chair and crossed his arms over his chest. "I know it's hard on you being away from the men you care for. There's no reason you can't go spend the night with them—"

"Right, because driving an hour after working all day then getting up at three-thirty in the morning in order to be here by five is so doable." Not to mention, she'd get no sleep at all. As much as she'd been missing Justin and Evan, they'd fuck until she had to leave.

Chance's dark eyebrows scrunched together as he frowned. "They're an hour away? Which ranch—" His eyes widened as realisation dawned.

Annabelle swallowed down her nervousness as she nodded. "Yeah, the Silver Spur ranch."

"You know, all I can think is *duh*." Chance shook his head. "I don't know many people out here, so I should have connected your Justin with Josh's brother. Shit, I feel like an idiot."

"Well, don't. I wasn't sure how you or Rory would react and didn't want either of you being pissed at Josh. He didn't exactly encourage me to hook up with Justin and Evan."

"I feel a little better."

Annabelle turned enough to look at her brother standing in the doorway. "Didn't you learn not to eavesdrop the other day?"

Rory rolled his eyes and walked into the office. He propped a hip on Chance's desk as he faced her. The sad expression was one Annabelle had seen on her brother's face almost continually the past several days, but the guilt in his midnight blue eyes was new. "What I've learned is that you don't think you can talk to me, confide in me, and I admit I haven't made it easy. The way I reacted to finding out about your, um, relationship, was proof enough of that."

Annabelle blinked frantically against the moisture pooling in her eyes as she glanced at the floor. "I didn't try to talk to you, even, so it's not like it's all your fault."

"But I wouldn't have reacted any better," Rory admitted gruffly. "I know I'm a prude—"

Chance snorted with enough melodrama that both Annabelle and Rory chuckled. "Okay, I'm a prude about *some* things, but the truth is, I shouldn't confine you to what is right for me, which is a monogamous relationship with the only man I'll ever love. That's wrong for me to do, and I'm really sorry."

Annabelle looked up to find her brother pushing away from the desk. She stood and opened her arms and couldn't hold back a quiet sob as Rory's strong arms enfolded her. Annabelle buried her head against her brother's chest and held on to the one man she'd always been able to count on. They both might falter here and there, but when it came down to it, they would always have each other's backs.

"I just want you to be happy," Rory whispered in her ear. "And if it takes two men or a dozen of them to do that, then it's fine with me."

"I think…I think it's more than just them making me happy," Annabelle confessed, "I think I need them both."

Rory sighed as his big body shuddered, and he hugged her tight before stepping back, catching her hands in his. "Then you go to them. We'll see about hiring someone else to come in and work early morning if we need to on the nights you stay with your guys. Maybe they can even stay a few nights with you at the bunkhouse, though I don't know what their situation is at their ranch."

Chance had started snickering before Rory finished, and Annabelle peered around Rory's arm to glare at the older man. Rory twisted around to look at Chance as well. "What?" Rory asked, "What'd I say?"

But Annabelle knew, from the way Chance's eyes were lit with devilment and his lips tipped up in a smirk. She glared at him and willed him to incinerate on the spot if he said anything to her brother, at least before she got the hell out of the room.

"Tell you in a bit," Chance said as he winked at them. "Otherwise your sister is gonna kick my ass 'til it's sitting on my shoulders."

"Already is," Annabelle muttered. Rory chuckled and patted her back.

"Nah, sis," he mock-whispered, "trust me, his ass is even finer than his face."

"Ew." Annabelle crossed her eyes at Chance. "That's TMI."

"Sounds about like what—"

Annabelle tipped her head down as she looked at Chance, who just grinned and winked again.

"You go on, Annabelle, we'll cover your chores in the morning, and come up with a working solution for all of us. Go on and git."

Annabelle hugged her brother again then practically ran around the desk to hug Chance as well. "You're gonna narc on me, aren't you?"

"Only a little," Chance admitted. "No sense in traumatising your brother."

"Exactly." Annabelle said her goodbyes and even if she did force herself to walk towards the bunkhouse, inside she was skipping and saying screw dignity. She was finally going to see her men.

Rory watched Annabelle leave, noting the lack of tension in her step that'd been evident to him since she'd returned. "I'm gonna lose her, aren't I?"

"Oh, no baby, no," Chance said, and Rory sighed as Chance's arms came around him, pulling his back against Chance's chest. "You won't ever lose her as long as you love her enough to accept her."

"But she's gonna leave, eventually, and move in with those two guys," Rory muttered, hating the jealous bite to his voice. He wanted Annabelle to be happy, he just wanted her to be happy *here*.

Chance squeezed him hard and fast, a loving reprimand. "Those two guys have names, Justin and Evan, and I think they care about your sister as much as she cares for them. They'd be fools not to, and I don't think Annabelle's the type to tolerate a fool."

No, she wasn't, but still. Rory had figured out his anger was less from the fact his sister was seeing two men and more from the fact she hadn't felt she could confide in him, and rightfully so. But now Rory had the added fear of losing her, not permanently, but…

"You can't keep her here with you forever," Chance said, as if reading Rory's mind. "And at least she'll only be an hour away if she decides to make this relationship she's in permanent."

"You think it can work, two men and a woman?" Rory didn't want Annabelle hurt. He felt Chance nod, his lover's chin digging into Rory's shoulder.

"Yeah, I do. I think as long as the three of them love each other, and are dedicated to making it work, it can, and it will."

Rory didn't know what to say to that, so he turned in Chance's arms and crushed his lips against his lover's, needing to forget everything but Chance for a while.

"Anything you want," Chance breathed the words out against Rory's lips. "It's yours, sweetheart. I'm yours."

And Rory knew that would be more than enough to help him through whatever heartache he experienced when his sister finally decided to leave.

Epilogue

Maybe she should have called, warned the guys she was on the way. Her men hadn't been any happier about their separation than she had, but at least Justin and Evan had each other. She had had her damned vibrator and more phone sex than was humanly possible. The idea of popping up, surprising her lovers, led to a multitude of erotic fantasies that kept Annabelle's foot down on the gas pedal. She couldn't *wait* to see them, touch them, taste them...

"Oh God," Annabelle groaned as lust coiled tight and hot in her belly. Her entire body felt flushed, her nipples and sex pulsing with her heartbeat. At the rate she was going, she'd have both men pinned to the ground or whatever surface was available as soon as she saw them.

Annabelle yelped and swerved to avoid an armadillo. "The hell?" She hadn't seen one of the oddly cute critters before, at least not outside of a zoo. "No wonder if they like to play chicken with trucks." Although the speed the little bugger put on was impressive. Who knew something that looked like it wore plates of armour could run so fast?

The sighting of the armadillo served to distract Annabelle from her arousal for which she was grateful. She'd like to actually be able to tell Justin and Evan about Chance's proposition, and find out whether or not them staying over at the bunkhouse on occasion was doable or not.

They'd have to get earplugs for Bo and Max. Or maybe one of those wave-sound machines, with big speakers. Or earmuffs…

Annabelle cut the wheel for the turn onto the long drive to her lovers' home. With the sun setting almost directly behind the structure, the whole place had a warm glow that gave Annabelle a sense of peace just from looking at it. She slowed the truck down despite how anxious she was to see Evan and Justin. Wouldn't be much of a surprise if she came roaring down the drive, spewing rocks and dirt all over. Not that the diesel engine was quiet, but if the guys were still working, maybe they wouldn't hear it.

Annabelle put the truck in park and pulled the keys out. Before she unbuckled, the front door was flung open and a shirtless Evan ran out, leaping down the porch steps with a grin that would have put a certain fictional cat's to shame. He had her truck door open in time to reach out and lift her from the seat, then she was gasping as her back met the passenger door. She had a second to take in the want in Evan's eyes, then his mouth was on hers, a fierce press of lips and teeth, his tongue swooping in to lay claim to her secret spots.

Her ass was grabbed, her body lifted until her feet dangled above the ground as she clung to Evan's shoulders. The feel of his stiff cock pressing against the juncture of her thighs nearly singed her brain.

Annabelle moaned as she sucked on Evan's tongue, mimicking the action she longed to use on his shaft.

"Starting without me?"

Annabelle barely had time to register Justin's teasing question. Before she could answer, she was released, her feet briefly touching the ground before she was lifted again then pressed back against the truck as Justin took Evan's place. "Missed you, honey," Justin rasped, his dark eyes burning with the same need coursing through her. "Gonna show you how much."

Justin's kiss wasn't the rough plundering Annabelle expected. Instead her lips were gently sucked, her mouth tenderly invaded as Justin told her without words how much he wanted her, how much he needed her. Tears leaked from the outer corners of Annabelle's tightly closed eyes as she gave herself to Justin, knowing well he was claiming her in his own way, just as Evan had done moments before. How had she got so lucky as to find these two men? She'd never thought to settle down, yet now she could think of little else except being with her lovers.

"Let's get inside," Justin whispered against her lips. Annabelle nodded and whimpered as Justin slid her down the length of his body. He looped an arm through hers and Evan did the same on the other side.

Once inside, Annabelle found herself pinned between the two men. Evan gave her a heated look and muttered 'Sorry'. Before she could ask why, he gripped the collar of her shirt and slid his hands down to where the material was buttoned right above her breasts. Annabelle realised his intent too late. With a smug grin Evan grasped the cotton material and jerked, sending buttons pinging all over the entryway.

"Fuck yes." Evan helped her pull the shirt off as Justin's deft fingers worked her belt buckle. Evan leered then cupped her breasts in his hands before burying his face in her cleavage. Annabelle half expected a reference about how good it was to be king, but Evan was too busy licking and sucking up marks on her milky white skin.

Justin tugged and Annabelle's belt, jeans, and underwear were around her thighs. "Needa get your boots off," Justin pointed out, and Annabelle would have agreed but Evan bit one nipple while pinching the other hard enough to be well and truly felt through her bra. Annabelle gasped and arched her back, thrusting her chest forward in a plea for more. Her bare ass met bare flesh as Justin's thick rod pressed between the cheeks of her ass, riding her crease and driving her mad.

"God, please," Annabelle panted, all thoughts of conversation forgotten as her body was stimulated unbearably. "Please, Justin, Evan—"

Evan responded by lifting her bra and feasting on her tits, giving her the sharp, pain tinged bites and hard sucks she needed. Justin pumped harder against her ass, then fitted his dick between her thighs so that his length rubbed against her cunt and asshole. *Yes!* Annabelle nearly came as Justin's cockhead nudged her ring. Hadn't Evan said when Justin took her like that, it'd be another claiming, that once he'd had her ass, he'd own it? Instead of freaking Annabelle out, she craved the invasion, more for what the act would mean than for the physical pleasure she knew she'd get from it.

"Bedroom, now," Evan rasped after another nip that left Annabelle weak in the knees. They paused long enough to strip off the rest of their clothes, then they made their way to the bedroom, the short walk hampered by their need to touch and kiss. Annabelle's breasts were treated to more of Evan's loving, and her pussy was filled with fingers and, at one point, Justin's tongue as he stopped and pressed her forward, placing her hands on the wall so he could bury his face in her sex. He sucked and pinched at her labia then thrust his tongue into her folds. When he dragged that slick muscle back until he laved over her pucker, Annabelle screamed and pushed her butt against his face, seeking the promised penetration.

Justin's gruff chuckle vibrated from her ring up to her spine then spread heat throughout her body. He clutched her cheeks and spread them wide, then entered her rosette with one firm press of tongue. His hand slid around to pluck at her clit, and Annabelle came on a scream as pinpoints of pleasure exploded into an ecstasy that rocked every nerve in her body.

"Now let's get to the bed," Justin purred as he stood and pulled her back to his chest. Annabelle wasn't sure she could walk, and so she didn't snap her lover's head off when he lifted her and carried her to the bedroom. "Get the stuff," Justin ordered, and Annabelle was dimly aware of Evan hustling to follow Justin's command.

Justin lowered her to the bed, settling her on her back. He came down on her in a smooth move, propping himself on his forearms as his muscular body covered her. "You're not leaving us."

Annabelle wished she could give him the answer he wanted, but she had obligations she couldn't easily dismiss, and the three of them needed time to develop what was growing between them. But she could commit to working towards what he wanted.

"I have to," Annabelle began, then stopped to grab two handfuls of Justin's hair when he would have pulled away. "I can't just leave my job, you should both understand that. But Chance and Rory, even Bo and Max, are willing to help us out. I can come in later in the mornings, and if y'all are able, you and Evan could stay a couple of nights with me in the bunkhouse. We could take a little time to make sure—"

"We're sure!" Evan and Justin both said loudly enough so that Annabelle's temper spiked. She glared at Evan first, then Justin as she tightened her hold on his hair until he winced.

"And so am I, but that doesn't mean we can't take the time to strengthen our relationship before I move in here with you two."

Justin's grin was slow in coming, but it reached his eyes, and the anger she'd seen in their depths turned into that molten look that caused her cunt to cream.

"I'm not running anymore," Annabelle explained as her heartbeat sped up. "But you and Evan need to respect that I have other responsibilities and I can't just walk away from them."

"But you *want* to be with us," Evan pressed, lying on the bed so that his head was beside hers. He gave her that look, the one that made her gooey inside and want to give him whatever he asked for. "You'll move in with us soon, make this official?"

Annabelle didn't know about soon—she was pretty sure their idea of soon would be different from hers—but she'd do it when she thought the time was right, which is what she told them. Both men studied her for a moment, and though they weren't pleased, they weren't angry. Annabelle understood their inclination to pin her down and make her commit to moving in with them as soon as possible, and she loved them both for giving her the time she needed even though they wanted more.

Not that she would tell them she loved them just yet. If she did, they'd do everything they could to convince her to stay with them, and Annabelle was afraid she'd give in despite her other responsibilities. Besides, she needed some time to get used to that revelation herself before she blurted it out.

"Kiss me," she ordered, not caring which man did it, so long as one of them kept her from talking. Evan groaned and cupped her cheeks, pulling her head around for a kiss that had Annabelle's eyeballs rolling back in her head. Or maybe that was due to Justin, who was nibbling and kissing his way down her chest. He sucked one sensitive nipple in his mouth as Evan swiped his tongue over the roof of her mouth and Annabelle knew then it was both men driving her closer to the edge she'd just recently tumbled over.

Justin let her nipple go with a lewd pop, then continued trailing a path of kisses down until he reached her clit. He scraped his teeth over the bundle of nerves and Annabelle arched into the touch. Evan's nimble fingers tugged and rolled her nipples and Annabelle writhed, trying to get a firmer touch on the hot spots her men were tormenting. Justin sucked her clit into his mouth and rolled his tongue over it as Evan bit her bottom lip and gave her taut peaks the attention they needed. Annabelle gasped and thrashed as she came again, her muscles clenching and spasming from the intensity of her climax.

"That's it, baby, just like that," Justin crooned. He licked down her slit, delving his tongue into her cunt for a quick fuck, then licked lower as he grasped her thighs and shoved her legs up.

Evan rolled over and Annabelle would have asked what the hell he was doing, stopping now, but Justin's tongue dragged over her pucker and Annabelle couldn't think, much less speak. She closed her eyes and grabbed handfuls of the blanket as Justin began eating her ass, priming her for what was soon to come.

"Lift up, honey," Evan said, but he was further away from her than he'd been and Annabelle knew he wasn't talking to her. She felt the bed shift as Justin moved, then heard the crinkle of a wrapper being torn open. The sound of skin on skin followed, then a moan against her opening. Annabelle lifted her head and forced her eyes open to find Justin on all fours between her legs, Evan reaching under him to roll on a condom. Justin moaned again as he thrust into Evan's hand. Evan chuckled and released the thick cock.

"Ah ah, I think there's something you want more than my hand." He popped open the lube and squirted some on his fingers before holding the tube out to Justin. "Do yourself while I get her ready for you."

Justin buried his tongue in deep one last time before planting a kiss on her hole and sitting up on his knees. He took the lube and began coating his sheathed dick as Evan scooted up to Annabelle's hip and pressed the tip of one finger to her pucker. He looked at her with an expression of concern as he rubbed at the ring of muscles.

"Have you ever done this before?"

Annabelle tried to speak but only managed to whimper. She settled for a nod.

Evan smiled slyly as he pushed his finger into her ass. "But not like Justin's gonna do you."

She didn't doubt it. The two or three times she'd had anal before hadn't particularly been memorable. None of the men had been anywhere near as well-endowed as Justin.

Evan turned to watch his finger pumping in and out of her body as Annabelle lay back and closed her eyes. She'd loved to have watched, but it wasn't comfortable. They needed mirrors, those tacky kinds on the ceiling or something. A burning sensation spread up her rectum from her pucker, and she knew Evan had worked another finger into her.

"Look at you," she heard Justin mutter, and she made a mental note to ask about mirrors. "Fuck that's pretty."

"Gonna be prettier in a minute," Evan said as the pressure around her pucker increased. The pain was sharper, less a burn and more just hurt, but Annabelle welcomed it. The first time she'd done this, the guy hadn't prepared her, and she sure as hell hadn't known any better. She was lucky he had a dick the size of one of those little canned sausages, or else she might never have tried this again. Annabelle opened her eyes, ready to plead for Justin and Evan to fuck her, but Justin must have read her body's need.

"That's enough." Justin traced his fingers around her opening, still filled with Evan's digits. With his other hand gripping the back of Evan's neck, he drew Evan to him for a rough kiss, almost more of a fight for dominance than a show of affection, and it turned Annabelle on more than she'd thought possible.

When Justin ended the kiss, Evan withdrew his fingers from her pucker then sprawled beside her on the bed on his back. He stroked his dick, which Annabelle realised was sheathed. Both of them, then. Oh God, she nearly burst into flames at the thought.

"Need you, Belle," Evan whispered.

Annabelle rolled to her side, then carefully straddled Evan's knees. She bent forward and nuzzled his balls, wishing she'd had the chance to suck his big dick before he put on the condom. Evan grunted and reached for her arms, his eyes laden with desire.

"Belle, please."

Annabelle scooted up as Justin stroked her back, her hips, her ass. She grasped Evan's cock, keeping her gaze locked with his, and lined it up with her wet pussy. Evan let go of her arms and clutched her hips, his breath coming in short, rapid bursts. Annabelle smiled and rubbed the fat crown into her juices, then when Evan opened his mouth to plead for more, she slammed herself down, filling her cunt with the thick shaft.

Evan's howl, the bruising strength of his fingers, only fanned the flames of Annabelle's arousal. She didn't give him or herself a minute to adjust, instead riding his dick hard and fast, ramming her ass down, stuffing herself over and over as Evan gasped and moaned, his hips jerking as he matched her frantic rhythm.

Justin moved in behind her, and Annabelle stilled as he clasped her chin, turning her head for a kiss that had her bucking her hips. Justin licked her lips then placed his hand between her shoulder blades and gently pushed her forward until her breasts pressed against Evan's chest. Evan immediately tangled his fingers in her hair and took over the kissing. Annabelle moaned into the kiss as she felt Justin pry her butt cheeks apart. The blunt fat crown brushed over her pucker and Annabelle tried to scoot back only to find herself held by Evan's hands twined in her hair.

When Justin gripped her hip with one hand, Annabelle could have wept with relief. The press of his tip into her tight ring had her eyes burning as much as her ass, but God, she wanted him, them, wanted Evan and Justin for as long as she could have them. Her nails scored Evan's biceps as Justin pushed in further. Again she tried to rock back into the penetration only to find herself unable to do so.

"You need more?" Justin rasped even as he pressed in deeper.

Annabelle arched her back as much as she could in answer. Justin gripped both hips then plunged forward until his balls slapped against her. Annabelle jerked her lips from Evan's to shout her pleasure as she was stretched until she felt she'd burst. It hurt, but nowhere near an intolerable level, and really, as Annabelle was learning about herself, she did seem to like a rough bite of pain at times.

And Justin seemed to know when that was, as did Evan. Giving her a moment to adjust, Justin added his finger bruises to Evan's on her hips. He ground his groin against her ass, working his dick in deeper, stretching her pucker even wider. Then with a strangled shout he began to fuck her.

Grunts and groans, bodies slapping and flesh sliding as sweat pooled and ran over them. Annabelle couldn't do more than hold on as Justin pounded into her ass and Evan fucked her pussy in short hard strokes. Her body was suffused with so much pleasure, almost more than she could bear as Justin dropped down over her, catching himself on his hands as he pumped his dick into her. Evan let loose a garbled scream as Justin's shift in position caused his cock to rub against Evan's more forcefully through the thin wall separating her entrances. His entire body jerked as Annabelle felt his cum spurt inside her despite the condom.

Evan shivered and Justin wrapped his arms around Annabelle's body, cupping her breasts as he pulled her up until they were both on their knees. Evan scooted up until his back was braced by the headboard, then he gave her a satisfied smile that seemed to say *now you're in for it!*

A nudge from Justin had Annabelle dropping back down, her head resting on her folded arms over Evan's thighs, then her eyes shot wide open as Justin began to fuck her with the strength she'd seen him fuck Evan with. Heat spiralled up from her ass, shooting through her rectum and burning pathways to her extremities. Her spine tingled and her head felt light. Justin slammed into her, his hips slapping her ass, his balls slapping her cunt, and all Annabelle could do was gasp as Justin took her, marking her with the force of his need as surely as if he'd branded her.

One big hand came down to hold the back of her neck as Justin's used his other hand to flick her clit. Ecstasy coiled in Annabelle's belly, spreading to her womb. Justin pressedher pearl harder as he ploughed into her, and Annabelle's climax tore into her and rendered her speechless, breathless, as she quivered and gave herself over to her men.

"That's it, honey," Justin ground out, then he speared her deeper than he had yet. His big body stilled as his cock swelled inside her, then he moaned as he came, his thick length pulsing several times as he found his release.

Justin withdrew and tumbled to the bed, dragging Annabelle with him so that she lay between him and Evan. Annabelle cupped each of her lovers' hands where they rested on her belly. Her body ached in a well-used way she wished she could feel forever, but as her neck and lips were nuzzled and kissed,

Annabelle knew she'd have a lifetime with Evan and Justin to bask in the warmth of their love.

About the Author

A native Texan, Bailey spends her days spinning stories around in her head, which has contributed to more than one incident of tripping over her own feet. Evenings are reserved for pounding away at the keyboard, as are early morning hours. Sleep? Doesn't happen much. Writing is too much fun, and there are too many characters bouncing about, tapping on Bailey's brain demanding to be let out.

Caffeine and chocolate are permanent fixtures in Bailey's office and are never far from hand at any given time. Removing either of those necessities from Bailey's presence can result in what is know as A Very, Very Scary Bailey and is not advised under any circumstances.

Bailey Bradford loves to hear from readers.

You can find her contact information, website details and author profile page at http://www.total-e-bound.com

Total-E-Bound Publishing

www.total-e-bound.com

Take a look at our exciting range of literagasmic™
erotic romance titles and discover pure quality
at Total-E-Bound.

www.ingramcontent.com/pod-product-compliance
Lightning Source LLC
Chambersburg PA
CBHW030320180626
46810CB00003B/1168